Acquiring the Cowboy Billionaire

A Chappell Brothers Novel: Bluegrass Ranch Romance Book 6

Emmy Eugene

CHAPTER 1

Duke Chappell stood in the line to walk down the aisle, one of Ginny's second cousins on his arm. He glanced at the woman, but he'd already forgotten her name. That was saying something for a man like Duke, who'd learned long ago how to memorize names —especially female names—because he was always ready to ask someone out if they interested him.

The problem was, no one interested Duke half as much as Lisa Harvey.

She wasn't at today's wedding, because she had no reason to be. He wasn't dating her, despite the tender moments they'd shared on Thanksgiving Day, a little over three weeks ago now.

He couldn't stop thinking about her, though, and his feet shifted as if he'd leave his brother's wedding and drive to her farm to make sure she was okay.

She hadn't stopped by his office at all, and she hadn't texted him beyond the business they needed to talk about.

Frustration built inside him as the music started. Everyone in line perked up a little, and Duke was eternally glad in moments like these that he sat at the end of the Chappell family and not the beginning.

Being the youngest hadn't always been easy for Duke, but he'd grown into the role. At some point a year or two ago, he'd realized that he didn't have to be the loudest or best to be valuable, both on the ranch and in his family. He didn't have to ask every woman for her number, and he didn't have to go out with them all either.

He'd dated enough now to know what he liked, and he knew he gravitated toward a woman with dark hair and dark eyes, as they held more mystery for him than blondes. He liked women who could talk to him without being awkward, and he didn't say no to a woman who knew how to cook, dance, and make him laugh.

He didn't think he'd put in too tall of an order with the Lord, but he sure hadn't had much luck finding someone he wanted to walk down the aisle with. Not the way Cayden and Ginny had. With Lawrence announcing his proposal on the family text only minutes ago, Duke's collar felt far too tight in a way that wasn't all physical.

He still reached up to try to loosen it, swallowing when he had a little bit more room between his Adam's apple and his bowtie. Cayden and Ginny's wedding was extremely formal, which didn't fit either of them all that well. But it fit their outside personas, and every groomsman wore a full tuxedo with tails.

Duke felt like a complete idiot, because he was about as far from a tuxedo as Pluto was from the sun. When he got married, he wanted to be in jeans and a plaid shirt, riding a horse, with his bride on a horse at his side. He didn't care what she wore, and he wanted to ride past his friends and family while they cheered and let off balloons.

Then the pastor would marry them, and he and his new bride would ride into the sunset and live happily-ever-after.

The whole thing would take a week to prepare, and about a half an hour to execute, and then he'd be done.

Duke didn't have the patience for a long engagement and huge, drawn-out celebration. He believed in marriage, and he did want to get married. He just didn't understand the show behind it. To him, it was a colossal waste of time, energy, and money, and all of those were finite.

He turned to the woman on his arm, and she wore a sparkly, gold dress that fell all the way to the floor. All women wore heels with a dress like that, and he gave her a smile. "I've got you, okay? You ready?"

She smiled back at him and nodded, her nerves plain in her eyes.

Duke had been in three weddings now, and he'd made this walk before. He put a smile on his face and took the first steps when he needed to, glad he'd worn his black cowboy dress boots with his tux. He, Ian, and Spur were the only ones who'd refused to trade out their boots for shiny loafers. Daddy too. The man hadn't worn anything but cowboy boots for fifty years, and it didn't matter if it was literally the biggest wedding the entire state of Kentucky had ever seen.

The aisle went on and on, and the faces started to blur after the first three steps. Duke kept going until he reached the altar, where Cayden stood in his tuxedo. He didn't look nervous at all, but he had a special way of stuffing everything away where no one could see it.

The music switched from the frilly, classical sounds that had been twinkling through the hall to the wedding march. Duke turned his attention to the back of the room where he'd tromped into the hall, expecting to see Ginny.

She didn't appear, and her father had died years ago. She'd asked Daddy to walk her down the aisle, and Duke's father had been riding that high for months now. He didn't have any girls of his own to walk down the aisle, and Ginny had literally made all of his dreams come true with a simple question.

The crowd grew somewhat restless, which honestly wasn't hard to do when a thousand people needed to be entertained and catered to.

Then a murmur rose up, and that turned into a cry. Duke saw several people pointing, and he too craned his neck to look up.

A part of the ceiling had detached and was slowly sinking toward the floor.

Ginny rode on it by herself, holding onto a pole to keep herself steady. She wore a snow-white dress that clung to her curves in a way that only custom-made clothing could do.

Lace covered the bodice and ran up past the white fabric

that covered her to her shoulders and down to her wrists. Her skin could peek through that lace, and she looked like an angel descending from heaven to marry her cowboy.

Duke could admit he was impressed by that, and he couldn't stop smiling as the platform reached the ground and Ginny reached for Daddy. He'd somehow appeared right where he needed to be, and he grinned at her as they started a limping step toward Cayden.

The platform had brought Ginny two-thirds of the way to the altar, so they didn't have to walk far. Daddy pressed his cheek to Ginny's and then passed her to Cayden, who kissed her against the corner of her eye and faced the altar.

Duke's relief soared through him as he got released from his brotherly duties of standing in a rainbow around the altar. He took small steps as he shuffled with everyone else, finally taking his seat on the end of the front row, on the far right. He could barely see Cayden and Ginny because of the width of this place, but he was determined to pay attention to his brother's nuptials.

He'd been making a conscious effort to stay off his phone more, because it was seriously his default for anything. Standing in a line at the store? He was on his phone. He'd just finished a class? Time to check his phone. Talking to Lawrence in the office they shared? He could scroll social media or answer texts at the same time.

Sometimes he hated his phone, and he hadn't even brought it into the hall for the wedding.

At the altar, the pastor gave a sweet speech about relying on each other and finding ways to show love for one another on a daily basis. Cayden and Ginny were the perfect example of relying on each other, as Duke had observed Cayden making the thirty-minute drive to Ginny's rental house whenever she needed him. He'd pack up his work and take it with him, because he wanted to be the safest, softest place for the woman he loved.

Duke wanted to be that man for someone too, and his thoughts went right back to Lisa. He frowned at himself as Cayden turned toward Ginny, and she started reading her vows.

"Cayden, you captured my heart long before I was even ready to give it away. You've always been there for me when I needed it, and I love that I can depend on you for anything, at any time." She smiled at him, and the power of it filled the entire space from top to bottom. She really possessed a strong spirit, and Duke had always liked her.

Ginny and Cayden had told him and Lawrence not to plan on moving out of the homestead. It was a huge space, with six bedrooms, and they didn't mind sharing two of them upstairs.

Duke really didn't want to live there with them alone, and depending on when Mariah and Lawrence got married, he might have to make some new living arrangements in the very near future.

"I love you with my whole heart today," Ginny said. "It only grows with each passing day, and I promise to be by your side for all of the steps of your life. Good days, and bad ones. All the pretty things, and all the ugly ones too." She beamed at her husband-to-be, and Duke had the distinct thought that Cayden was the luckiest man in the world. "I'm thrilled I get to be your wife, and bear your name."

"Wow," the pastor said. "I don't know how Cayden is going to top that."

The crowd twittered with laughter, and Duke's mind took a moment to catch up. He laughed a little bit too late, and he cut off his voice when everyone else started to as well. He didn't need his loud voice echoing in this hall during his brother's wedding.

"Virginia," Cayden said, lifting her hands to his lips. "You are the love of my life, and I've known it almost from the moment I met you. I would do anything for you, and I can't wait to experience our life together."

He turned back to the pastor, his promise short and sweet. Even getting him to say his vows into the microphone had not been something he'd wanted to do, but he'd spoken the truth when he'd said he'd do anything for Ginny.

The pastor used the powers vested in him from God above and the state of Kentucky, and he pronounced Cayden and Ginny man and wife.

The crowd surged to their feet, and Duke was once again caught off-guard. He did stand and start clapping, but he didn't join his loud cowboy voice to the rest of his family on the front row. Several of them whistled through their teeth —something Duke could do too—but he didn't do that either.

Cayden dipped Ginny right there at the altar and kissed her, which only prompted more and rowdier cheering.

Then they turned toward the crowd and lifted their

joined hands. They walked down the aisle, running the last few steps to the platform. They both got on this time, and with one hand secured to the pole, they waved with their free hand to everyone gathered in the hall.

The life in the party left with them, and Duke turned to Lawrence. "That was pretty amazing."

"Spectacular," his brother agreed.

"Are you going to do something like that for your wedding?"

"I doubt it," Lawrence said, smiling at Duke. "You?"

"I can't even imagine getting married inside," he said. He didn't make it a well-known fact that he'd thought about his wedding day, because that apparently wasn't something men did. He just knew he didn't want a big fuss.

"Let's go get something to drink before the luncheon," Lawrence said, leading the way down the aisle.

Duke followed him back to the reception room, where the refreshments had been replenished. He took a moment to pick up his phone from where he'd placed it in the windowsill. His heartbeat caught in his throat when he saw Lisa had texted him.

Not only that, but she'd called too.

He tapped on her name to read her text, and she'd said, *My daddy has gone into the hospital. Can you call me when you get a minute?*

He glanced around, wondering if this was the right minute to introduce this emergency into his life. Should he call now or wait until the wedding festivities were over?

He hurried over to Daddy and showed him the phone. "Should I call her right now?'

"Yes," Daddy said. "Duke, there's one thousand people here. If you need to leave, no one's going to miss you."

"The most important thing that needed to happen today," Mom added. "Has happened." She linked her arm through Daddy's and leaned her cheek against his bicep. "Poor Wayne. I hope he's okay."

Duke knew he wasn't okay, and as he dialed Lisa, he prayed with all the energy of his soul that Wayne Harvey had had enough time to update his will.

CHAPTER 2

Lisa Harvey stood in the back of the microscopic hospital room, thinking that everything she'd seen on TV movies about the health care system had been wrong. There were no beeping machines assuring her that Daddy was still alive. The rooms weren't big enough to host families. The lighting was super harsh—none of this low lighting where female patients fell in love with handsome doctors.

In fact, the last three doctors that had been in the room had all been at least a decade younger than Lisa. At least. The last guy—a urologist—looked like he was barely fourteen years old. And none of them had been tall, dark, and handsome.

They also didn't wear white coats with stethoscopes around their necks, and Lisa scoffed under her breath as she glanced toward her two half-brothers. Kelly and Bruce had huddled near the door of the room, and with their heads bent together, Lisa folded her arms and scowled in their direction.

They were likely talking about her. She wanted to talk to them and find out why they'd turned vitriolic toward her the moment Daddy had been diagnosed. That was the only thing that had changed in their family, and Lisa didn't understand the sudden shift.

It had happened to everyone—the brothers and their wives. Even the three nieces and nephews Lisa loved had turned somewhat cold toward her.

If she didn't love Daddy with her whole heart, and she didn't enjoy working with the horses quite so much, Lisa would leave Dreamsville. Her dreams certainly weren't coming true here, and she stood to lose everything she'd spent the last thirty-four years of her life working toward.

Familiar desperation swirled within her now, and no amount of swallowing and throat-clearing would make it go away. She'd been so desperate thirty minutes ago—*so* close to tears—that she'd texted Duke Chappell.

Her phone currently sat in her back pocket, and she'd left the notifications on, vibrations and everything. Daddy couldn't hear much without his hearing aids, and he hadn't turned them on that morning. There hadn't been time.

When Lisa had come in from her morning chores, she'd realized immediately that something was wrong. It was the lack of the scent of coffee hanging in the air. Daddy adored coffee, and he brewed his specialty grounds every morning by seven, no matter what.

Except there was a "no matter what," and it was that

Daddy hadn't been able to get out of bed that morning. Lisa had instantly gone down the hallway to his bedroom, calling his name. She could admit she'd hesitated at the closed door, wondering if she was going to find a breathing body on the other side...or one that wasn't.

She could still keenly feel the pinch of helplessness and the way her heartbeat had become a living, breathing, physical entity reverberating through her whole body. It had settled back into something she didn't even think about or detect, but for a few painful seconds standing in the hallway outside Daddy's bedroom, her pulse had consumed her.

He'd been alive, obviously, and he'd managed to get himself sitting up. He hadn't been able to get his right leg to move, though, and that meant he couldn't stand, couldn't walk, and couldn't make coffee.

His lack of caffeine had made him extremely unpleasant, and he'd barked at Lisa that she didn't need to fuss over him. She'd barked right back that someone needed to, and Bruce and Kelly weren't going to do it. Instant regret had filled her —still did—and she'd apologized profusely before calling both of her brothers to come help her.

Daddy was a big man, with a big personality. He'd been a cowboy his whole life, and he knew the value of hard work. Everything he had, he'd built.

Getting him to come to the hospital in an ambulance had been terribly difficult, and in the end, it had been Lisa who'd helped him see there was no other way.

You can't walk, Daddy, she'd said. *You know there's some-*

thing wrong. Something we don't know about yet. Why can't we go to the hospital and find out what it is?

She knew why he was resistant to doing such a thing.

Fear.

Fear was a very tangible being in Lisa's life, and it had been for the past seven months. It could coil around her heart and start to squeeze before she recognized it. It could seep under the cracks in the doors she'd been slamming closed for months. It could sneak up on her while she worked with a horse or shoveled out a stall, when everything had been sunny and perfectly fine only the moment before.

Right now, fear had a chokehold on her, and Lisa could barely get enough air into her lungs.

Her phone buzzed and zinged out a loud chime, drawing the attention of both brothers and Belinda, Bruce's wife, who sat in the only chair in the room. The three of them frowned at her simultaneously, as if receiving a message in the hospital was the worst possible crime on the planet.

"Who is it, baby?" Daddy asked. "Is it your momma, askin' 'bout me?" His words slurred slightly, and while Lisa couldn't see his face from her position in the back corner of the room, she didn't think he'd have his eyes open.

She also had no idea what to say. Her mother had left Dreamsville when Lisa was fifteen years old. She'd packed two suitcases and set them in the kitchen Lisa still used each morning. She'd gone about her day, making breakfast and weeding a flowerbed. When Daddy had come in from his chores, she'd announced she was leaving.

She hadn't offered to take Lisa with her, and Lisa

wasn't sure what she'd have done. In the first few months after her departure, Lisa had missed her terribly. Daddy had too. The two of them had clung to each other, and with Bruce and Kelly so much older than her, it had just been the two of them at the stud farm, working and grieving.

"I don't know, Daddy," she said quietly, pulling her phone from her pocket. She quickly pushed the sliding button up to put the device on vibrate-only, because she didn't need six eyes latching onto her and trying to fillet her alive. She also didn't need more questions like the one her daddy had just asked.

She hadn't heard from her mother in about five years now, and the only reason Darla had called last time was to tell Lisa that she'd gotten engaged to someone else. Her third marriage. Lisa had not attended the wedding, and she hadn't heard from her mother since.

The message was from Duke, and Lisa's heart grew a tiny set of wings. The man had some serious power over her, and she wasn't even sure when she'd opened the door and invited him into her life. They'd never gotten along all that well, but she suspected that was because of her saltiness toward him. He reflected it back to her, and she couldn't really blame him for that.

Sorry, he said. *I was in Cayden's and Ginny's wedding. I'm free now. I can call anytime. Tell me when.*

Lisa had forgotten about the wedding of the year, and foolishness filled her. She'd been disappointed and she'd started to see things through jade-colored glasses when Duke didn't pick up. He'd said she could call him and ask for anything, but he hadn't picked up.

She distinctly remembered scoffing and wishing she could take back the notification that would tell him she'd called and texted.

He'd been in a wedding, and Lisa swallowed the forming lump of embarrassment in her throat. There were going to be a lot of awkward and uncomfortable things she'd have to deal with in the near future. How she'd privately reacted to Duke not picking up her call was probably the smallest one.

She stepped over to the bed and gazed down at Daddy. "You're okay here for a minute, Daddy? It's Duke, and I need to call him back."

His eyes opened, and they looked like a newborn's eyes —unfocused and slightly watery. Daddy smiled and tried to reach his hand toward her. Lisa went most of the way and curled his fingers through his. "You rest," she said. "I'll be right back."

"Love you, baby doll," he said, his eyes drifting closed again. The moment froze, and Lisa was so glad there wasn't a horrible hospital machine beeping in this new memory. Daddy had always loved her, and after Mama had left, he'd tell her every night that they could get through hard times.

"Together, Lise," he'd said. "Me and you can do this. It's hard, and sometimes I want to raise my fist to heaven and ask God why this happened. What I did wrong."

She could still picture him shaking his head, such sorrow in his eyes. Then he flipped the chicken breast he'd been cooking and turned back to her. "But I love you, baby doll. At least she didn't take you from me too."

He'd become more affectionate after Mama had left, and Lisa hadn't hated that. He hugged her more often, and he'd put his arm around her and told her he was proud of her dozens of times since then.

She made it past the glaring bodyguards at the door and stepped into the hall. Relief hit her like a wall of water, and she stopped and blinked, trying to process so much in such a short space of time. She didn't want to go too far in case one of the doctors or nurses came back with news.

They'd sent Daddy for an MRI about forty minutes ago, and that was when Lisa's anxiety had overtaken her and she'd excused herself to call Duke.

As she dialed him now, she realized she just needed to hear a friendly voice, and his was the first she'd thought of. She just wanted someone who was on her side to tell her that she was a worthwhile human being.

She took a few steps away from the door and settled against the wall opposite of Daddy's room, tears already gathering in her eyes.

"Lisa," Duke said, his voice somewhat breathless. "Are you okay, honey?" He let the last word drip out of his mouth the way honey did, slow and sweet and delicious.

Lisa actually smiled, though she normally disliked terms of endearment that made her feel small or less-than who she was.

"Where are you?" he said. "I can change and be at the hospital in maybe thirty minutes."

She found she couldn't speak, not without revealing the emotions tumbling through her. *Would that be such a bad thing?* she wondered. She didn't let anyone in, except Daddy. He wasn't going to be with her much longer; she could simply feel it.

She drew in a deep breath, and said, "It's your brother's wedding, Duke. You can't just run out." Her voice was too high and somewhat strained, but every word she said helped her feel a little stronger.

"You'd be doin' me a favor," he said. "Everyone understands emergencies."

"This is *my* emergency," she said. "Not yours."

"Lisa," he said, but he didn't present another argument.

She looked down the hall, wishing the Lord would paint the words she should say on the stark walls. Maybe then she'd know how to talk to a man. Duke, specifically, she thought. Help me talk to Duke specifically.

"I'm okay," she said, pressing her eyes closed. "Daddy couldn't move his right leg this morning." The story poured from her in only a minute, and she took a long, shuddering breath when she finished.

"I'm so sorry, Lisa," Duke said, his voice soft and full of that caring compassion she'd seen on his face on Thanksgiving. "I'll come as soon as I can, okay?"

"Why?" she asked. "I haven't asked you to come."

He said nothing, and Lisa watched Daddy's nurse stand from the station down the hall. Her pulse bumped against her ribcage, and she straightened from the wall.

"I'm sorry to bother you on Cayden's wedding day," she

whispered. "Please forgive me. I just needed to hear a friendly voice, and yours was the first one I wanted to hear."

She had no idea what she'd really said between those words, but in that moment, she didn't care. "I just wanted someone to be on *my* side."

"I'm on your side," Duke said. "You don't have to do this alone, honey. I really will come."

She smiled. "I know," she said. "Thank you, Duke. The nurse is coming, and I have to go."

"Text me what you find out," he said. "I love your daddy too."

"Okay," she said, and armed with that knowledge that Daddy was loved by more than his family, Lisa stepped across the hall to arrive at the door of her father's room at the same time the nurse did.

She gave Lisa a smile and let her go in first. Lisa squeezed past Bruce and Kelly and returned to her spot near the back window. The cold air emanated off of the glass, and Lisa seized onto the sensation and let it move through her.

"The doctor just got the MRI scan," the nurse said. "He's on his way over. He shouldn't be long, but maybe another twenty minutes." She smiled at Daddy and went about her work checking things. What, Lisa didn't know.

She left the room again, and it was back to hurry-up-and-wait. Everything in the hospital happened on a molasses time schedule, with only microbursts of activity.

She re-pocketed her phone and sank into the counter.

The minutes passed slowly, and Lisa actually closed her eyes and rested her head against the window. The next time the door opened, a knock preceded it and then Duke Chappell's voice said, "Oh, this is the right room."

He entered without waiting to be invited in, and Lisa dang near fell down in her haste to straighten.

His eyes caught on hers, but Duke took a moment to say hello to her brothers, shaking both of their hands and saying he'd heard about Daddy and wanted to come see what the family needed.

He stopped at Daddy's bedside and leaned down to say something to him. Lisa couldn't hear anything through the fog that had enveloped her upon Duke's arrival. He wore a pair of blue jeans, a very shiny pair of black cowboy boots, and yellow polo that pulled across his chest. He'd covered that with a black leather jacket, and he was pure perfection in a cowboy hat.

Lastly, he turned his attention to her, taking the three steps past the bed to the tiny alcove which led into the even smaller bathroom. The sink was outside the bathroom, in the counter where Lisa had been attempting to doze.

"Hey, honey," he said quietly, sliding his arm around her waist and bringing her flush against his body. His touch melted all the icy pieces inside her. His care for her made her weep. She clung to him in a way she'd only done to Daddy before, and she allowed him to hold her up for several long moments while she couldn't do it herself.

"It's okay, now," he whispered, using one hand to stroke her hair. "I'm here now, honey, and you'll be okay."

She wasn't sure she believed him, but she wanted to. She seized onto the words and used them as a life preserver in this vast new ocean where she'd been trying to swim alone since May.

The door opened again, and Duke released her, both of them turning toward the door as the doctor entered. He took in the group of people, and even Belinda stood from the recliner, worry on her face.

The very room seemed to inhale and hold its breath while the doctor said, "We've got quite the crew in here." He smiled and looked at Daddy. "How are you feeling, Wayne?'

"I've been better," Daddy said, and Lisa couldn't hold back the half-sob, half-laugh.

"I'll bet you have," the doctor said. "Let's pull up your scan and see what you're dealing with."

Lisa couldn't see the computer screen from behind it, so she edged out, stealing Duke's hand so she could stay grounded. He went with her, and they moved to stand behind Daddy's bed, in the tiny space between it and the wall.

"Can you see?" Lisa whispered to Duke.

He shook his head and said, "It doesn't matter if I see, Lise. Can you see?"

She nodded, because the doctor had pushed the screen back so it was almost flat against the wall. She pulled in a breath and held it, then reached her free hand over the bed and put it on Daddy's shoulder.

He covered her hand with his, and they waited for the doctor to put the scan on the screen. Duke's hand in hers was tight and warm, and Lisa really liked it. She'd told him he shouldn't come, but he had anyway, and she liked that too.

She had to admit that she simply liked Duke Chappell, and maybe it was time to stop fighting the feelings that had been pinging at her for months now. She glanced at him, and when their eyes met, the charge that zapped between them could've revived Daddy's heart had he needed it.

She smiled, and Duke did too, and suddenly, Lisa could handle whatever image came up on the screen. Just like she'd had Daddy at her side when Mama had left, she now had Duke in her corner.

"Finally," the doctor said. "Here it is."

Lisa leaned over the bed a little more, as if getting closer to the screen would help her understand the image starting to form there.

"I'm afraid it's not good news," the doctor said, pointing with his pen. Lisa blinked, and the room turned white. The only thing anchoring her to the Earth was Duke's hand in hers.

CHAPTER 3

Duke didn't understand every word Dr. Bezzant said, but he knew the big ones. "Cancer," and "leukemia," and "kidney failure." None of those were good, and the masses on the MRI scan were so clear and so sobering.

Wayne Harvey had three tumors in his lungs, and Duke wasn't a medical doctor, but he knew that wasn't good. Beside him, Lisa sniffled every now and then while she listened. Bruce and Belinda asked most of the questions, and Duke noticed that Wayne didn't say anything.

He stared at the screen as if he couldn't believe what it was showing him. Duke couldn't look away from it, because the details were just so haunting.

"So." Dr. Bezzant took a deep breath and blew it out. "I'm going to get our pulmonary specialist in to see you, because he's the one that knows every pocket of the lung, and he'll know what we're dealing with far better than I will." He offered a smile, and to Duke's surprise, Wayne returned it.

The doctor said he'd go call the other doctor right now, and that he'd be by later that day. Duke knew what that meant for Lisa: more waiting. Not only that, but more waiting in this room with hostiles. He wasn't sure why Bruce and Kelly didn't like her, because he'd never gotten the vibe that they didn't get along.

Dr. Bezzant left, and the silence that descended into the room gnawed at his nerves. He felt very strongly that he should leave and let the Harveys discuss their sensitive family issues. He squeezed Lisa's hand and slipped his away. "I should go," he said.

"Tell your folks howdy for me," Wayne said, and Duke marveled at the kindness and strength of him.

"I will, sir."

"I'll send Lisa over with our card for Cayden and Ginny," he added, and Duke paused and turned back to him.

"I can come get it," he said. "Y'all have a lot going on right now." He looked from Wayne to Lisa, nodded, and reached past Bruce to leave the hospital room. If there was a worse feeling than walking away from Lisa Harvey and her sick father—and leaving them with wolves—Duke never wanted to feel it.

He paused, actually thinking he should go back, but he knew his family would want some privacy to discuss their health issues.

He made it to the elevators and reached to touch the

button. A sigh slipped out of his mouth, and he reached up to remove his hat and run his fingers through his hair.

"Duke."

He turned toward his name, the voice familiar. The brunette striding toward him made his heart thump when the sight of Lisa used to make him roll his eyes. "Hey," he said, stepping toward her. "You okay? I just didn't think I should stay."

She moved right into him and wrapped her arms around him. Her chest heaved against his, and Duke pressed his eyes closed and prayed that all of his strength could be transferred to her. "Shh," he soothed, but he didn't care if she kept crying or not.

The elevator dinged, and that caused Lisa to step back. "I won't keep you. Thank you for coming, Duke. Really." She wiped her eyes, but her dark lashes remained as black and as long as they always did.

"I'll come by tonight?" he asked. He'd probably have to answer to a few brothers, but he decided he didn't care. He didn't need to hide how he felt about Lisa Harvey, as they were both adults. He hadn't been out with anyone seriously since Allison Harrison, and that had been a little over a year ago.

Lisa nodded, and he drove back to Sweet Rose, where dinner had just started to be served when he'd left. All told, by the time he jogged back into the event hall where the nuptials had been exchanged, Duke had probably been gone for ninety minutes.

The family tables all sat at the front of the room, and

Duke was aware of all the eyes on him as he strode in that direction in his blue jeans. If this had been Spur's or Blaine's wedding, he might have gotten away with it, but Cayden demanded more refinement.

And Ginny? She was the definition of sophistication and superior class. She and Cayden were perfect for each other, but Duke would rather have a woman who wore cowgirl boots and wasn't afraid to break a nail while working out on the ranch.

He slid into his seat beside Trey, who raised his eyebrows and picked up Duke's unused fork. "Where you been?" he asked, handing Duke the utensil.

"Uncle Duke," TJ said, distracting both cowboys from the question at hand. "Did you get to ride the circle?"

Duke looked at Trey, who gestured behind them. "The platform up and down. While they were switching out the chairs for tables, they let some of the kids ride it up and down."

"Oh." Duke grinned at TJ and reached over to tousle the boy's hair. "No, buddy. I didn't get to ride that." He focused on his food, which had been sitting there unattended for a while. He had a bacon-wrapped filet mignon, spears of asparagus, and creamy mashed potatoes. Sweet Rose had their own kitchen, with a full-time chef on staff. They did plenty of events at the whiskey distillery, and they planned many more for the community.

Now that he was sitting, he didn't care what he was wearing. He'd just relaxed enough to cut a bite of steak and swipe it through his potatoes when Trey said, "And why didn't you get to ride the platform, Duke? Setting up too many chairs?"

He refused to look away from Duke, and his eyebrows only got higher with every passing second.

Duke wasn't going to get out of answering the question. He chewed slowly anyway, and though the meal was cold, it was still delicious. He swallowed and said, "A friend of mine had an emergency, and Daddy said I should go."

"On Cayden's wedding day?"

"Yep." Duke took another bite of steak and potatoes.

"Who's the friend?"

"Since when do you need to know everything?" Duke gave Trey a pointed look, and Trey only grinned at him. Lawrence certainly didn't help by stopping by the table and setting down a plate of cheesecake with raspberries spooned over the top of it.

"Thanks," Duke said.

"How's Lisa?" Lawrence asked.

Duke's eyes flew to Trey, whose smile only widened. "She's coping," Duke said.

"I tried to get you some chocolate cake, but they're restocking." Lawrence patted his shoulder and went over to his table.

"Lisa?" Trey asked. "Lisa Harvey? Pretty? Dark hair? Those big, brown eyes?" Trey fluttered his eyelashes, and his wife swatted at his arm.

"Leave the man alone," Beth said, grinning at Duke. "You're making his ears turn red."

"You can't see my ears," Duke said, rolling his eyes. He

did like Beth a lot, and she fit right into the Chappell family like a hole had been left just for her.

"Your face is turning red," she teased. "And I can see that."

"I'm sure it's not," Duke said. "I'm not embarrassed about Lisa Harvey."

"No?" Beth leaned her elbows on the table and rested her face in her hands. "Tell me about her. I don't know Lisa Harvey." She glanced at her husband, but where Trey had been so keen to jump in a few moments ago, he remained silent now.

"She owns Horses by Harvey," Duke said. "It's her father's company. They're a stud farm. We use a lot of their horses, and I've been working with Lisa on the scheduling for a couple of years."

"She's pretty?" Beth asked, glancing at her husband again.

Trey started to nod in an exaggerated way, and Beth swatted at him again. "Do you want to stay married?"

Trey burst out laughing, and Beth smiled, but Duke thought she wasn't kidding very much. Trey twisted away from Duke and put his arm around Beth, pulling her into his chest. He said something to her that Duke couldn't catch, and they laughed together.

"Dancing!"

Duke flinched away from the astronomical noise and the resulting interference coming through the speaker system.

"My word," Trey said.

"They're going to start cleaning up the tables," Beth said.

Duke started eating faster, and then he'd escape back to the reception room. He'd be able to ask for more dessert there, and he had no desire to dance with anyone...except Lisa Harvey, and she wasn't there.

* * *

Duke whistled while he opened the stall door and said, "Come on, Helena. Your turn to go out." The taupe-colored horse seemed to nod at him as she started walking, and he watched her go past him. "It's pretty muddy today," he told her. "You stay out of that, now, ya'hear?"

The horse went on by him and down the wide middle aisle toward Frieda, one of their equine specialists. Duke loved the job of letting the horses out of their stalls and into the pastures for the day.

They seemed to carry freedom in their manes and joy in their step. Some of them were a bit dodgy when they had to be herded back into the stables in the evenings, and some of them would need baths in the morning if they got too muddy today.

He closed the stall and moved to the next one. "All right, Hercules," he said. "You like to roll in the mud, but I really need you not to today, okay? You've got that trainer comin' in the morning, and we won't have time to give you a bath."

Hercules just looked at him with his big, doe-like eyes, gave a soft whinny, and headed out of the now-open gate.

The clomping of his hooves made Duke appreciate life, and he smiled at the tail-end of the horse.

One by one, he greeted the horses and let them out to pasture. "Got it," he said to Frieda, and the redhead nodded at him, gave him a shy smile, and turned to go attend to her next task. Duke watched her go, a twinge in his gut that he'd led her on and made her think he'd go out with her.

To be fair, he would've any other time, because Duke went out with everyone. Since Thanksgiving, though, his tune had changed, and he only wanted to see Lisa Harvey.

The last time he'd seen her was a week ago now, as he had gone over to the sprawling ranch house the night of Cayden's wedding, as promised. Lisa had been there alone, and he'd stayed with her for only a few minutes, taking the wedding card with him.

He still hadn't given it to Cayden, because the newly-weds were on their honeymoon and would be for another few weeks yet. Cayden had said Ginny just needed a break, and while they'd originally gone to California for their honeymoon, now they were simply hopping on any airplane, taking them anywhere they wanted to go.

Duke went to the doorway and leaned against it, the fresh air outside cleansing his lungs and centering his thoughts. He watched Frieda disappear into another stable, and he sighed, regret lacing through him.

He thought of Lisa's dark eyes, the tears caught in her eyelashes. He'd wanted to kiss them away and assure her once more that she'd be okay, no matter what. Truth be told, though, Duke had no idea what it would be like to be practically motherless since age fifteen, nor had he ever lost a parent.

Lisa had endured one of those, and from what Duke had seen on the MRI scan, she would definitely be losing her father in the near future. He reached for his phone, flipping it over and over in his palm, wondering if he should call her. He could ask how she was doing, and how her father had been doing since he'd left the hospital.

They'd put him on several medications, and when Daddy had come home from his hip surgery, Mom had said managing his care had been like a full-time job. So who was doing that for Lisa? Was she doing it? Was she still working the farm as much as she normally did?

Maybe she needed help, and guilt gutted him. "Stupid," he muttered. "You should've been over there every evening this week."

He lifted his phone to his ear after tapping her name and the phone icon, and the line rang and rang. Her voice mail picked up, and he said, "Lise, it's Duke. I'm gonna stop by in a little bit and see if you need any help, okay? I'm going right through town, so text or call if there's something you want me to pick up."

He hesitated, trying to decide what else to say. He finally just said, "Okay, bye," and hung up.

He checked the time on his phone and decided to go right then. He could stop at the grocery store and pick up a couple of freezer meals to take to her. Or, better yet, he could call Beth and ask her what she had in her freezer that Lisa might like. Certainly homemade freezer meals would be better than the prepackaged ones he could get from the case at the grocery store.

He dialed her and started back toward the homestead. He could clean up from his morning chores and stop by the Triple T Ranch on his way to Lisa.

"Duke," Beth said, surprise evident in her tone.

"Beth, howdy," he said. "I'm wondering if you have something in your freezer I can take to Lisa. I haven't heard from her all week, and I'm going over there to make sure she's okay."

"I've got chicken Alfredo," Beth said, her voice getting softer as she probably moved the phone away from her mouth. "I have minestrone soup. I have orange chicken. She can throw any of it in the slow cooker in the morning and have dinner when she comes in off the ranch."

"Would you mind if I took her a couple of things?'

"Of course not. Come by anytime. I'll put out a few things and put them in a cooler."

"Thank you, Beth." Armed with a plan, Duke hung up and hurried to the house. He washed up and grabbed his keys before jogging out to his truck. He stopped by Beth's and managed to avoid answering any questions as she'd left a note that said, *I had to go feed the calves. Good luck with your new girl, Duke.*

"Good luck," he muttered to himself, tucking the note into the cooler and leaving the big, white farmhouse where Trey lived with his family.

Duke made the drive to Lisa's farm and house, bumping down the gravel driveway about twenty minutes later.

Familiar trucks sat there—the same ones he'd seen on Thanksgiving Day.

His nerves jumped to the back of his throat, but he collected the cooler and headed for the front door, determined to see this through.

The doorbell sounded through the still countryside, and it almost felt too quiet to Duke. Too still, without even a winter breeze to kick its way through the surrounding fields.

Seconds ticked by, and Duke was about to leave the cooler and text Lisa when someone opened the door. A woman stood there, a generation older than Duke. "Hello," she said politely.

"Howdy, ma'am," he said. "I'm Duke Chappell. I'm wondering if Lisa is available?" He tried to see past the dark-haired woman, but she actually stepped further into the doorway, blocking his view almost completely.

She glanced down to the cooler. "What's in that?"

"Oh, I know her daddy's been sick," Duke said. "And I thought I'd bring some food, see how she was doing, how Wayne is, and see if I can help."

The woman wore a sympathetic look. "Honey, Wayne...died."

Duke blinked, trying to make sense of those three words. His chest felt hollow, his throat dry. His heart beat somewhere down in the bottom of his boots.

"He passed away early this morning," the woman added, her eyes falling to the porch at their feet. "Lisa probably just hasn't had the time or mental capability to tell you yet."

CHAPTER 4

Olivia Chappell had not slept well for weeks. She'd always carried a few extra pounds, but nothing like the bulging beach ball she'd been dealing with lately. She groaned as she rolled over, half-awake and desperately wishing she could go back to sleep.

"You okay, sweetheart?" Spur whispered from beside Olli. He threaded his fingers through hers, and the fact that he was still in bed told her the hour was still very early. He did go to work later in the winter, because there was no summer sun to beat, and Olli had enjoyed having him padding around their kitchen, making coffee and scrambled eggs, when she got out of bed.

"Mm." She squeezed his hand, because she couldn't really snuggle in closer to him the way she would've in the past. She kept her eyes closed and tried to drift back to sleep with Spur's added warmth nearby.

A few minutes later, he pulled his hand away and said, "I'm gonna shower."

Olli let him go without a word, because sometimes the sound of the shower could lull her back to sleep too. Spur half-closed the bathroom door, and a moment later, that telltale sound of water splashing down filled the air.

She must've fallen asleep, because the next time she woke, the house was silent. Half-desperate to go back to sleep and half-knowing something wasn't quite right, Olli held very still. Only the furnace hummed in the house, and she knew Spur had left to get to work on his sprawling horse ranch next door.

All at once, a cramping, tearing pain dove through her, and Olli realized what had woken her a few minutes ago.

She cried out at the contraction—or what she assumed was a contraction. She hadn't actually experienced one before, as this was her first baby, and she and Spur had fought like dogs to get it.

Putting both hands on her belly, she could feel the life inside her, and despite the pain, it made her smile. "Hold on, baby," she whispered to her infant. She just knew the baby would be a boy, but she and Spur had chosen not to find out the sex of the baby before now.

A strange sensation rolled across her stomach, as if someone had slid their hands across it and her flesh was rippling with the touch. With a grunt, Olli managed to push herself up and get her legs over the side of the bed.

Her phone sat on the nearby nightstand, and she quickly dialed her husband.

"Heya, Olls. I left breakfast on the stove. You were sleeping so soundly."

"The baby is coming," she said, though she should've thanked him for making breakfast and letting her sleep through it.

"Right now?" he asked.

Another contraction had her leaning forward as a tight, strained groan ground through her throat. "It feels like someone is trying to pull my spine out through my belly button," she said, panting. "I'm fairly sure it's a contraction."

"How close together are they?" he asked, his voice definitely on the upper range of panicked now.

"I don't know." Tears sprang to her eyes. "I woke up and laid here for a few minutes, because I can't really move, you know? Anyway, I had one, and I realized that had woken me up. And then I sort of had another one? I don't know. And then that one. So four in only a few minutes."

"I'm on my way back. You're okay to wait? Do I need to call an ambulance?"

"I can't imagine he'll come that fast," Olli said, and everything in her body seemed normal now. Maybe she'd hallucinated the contractions? Had she just called Spur back here for no reason?

"See you in a sec." The call ended, and Olli set her phone on the nightstand. Using it to support herself, she stood, taking a moment to make sure she could support her weight. She needed to use the restroom, and by trailing her hand along the bed and then the wall, she was able to get into the bathroom fairly quickly.

She took care of her business and turned to flush. A gasp flew from her mouth at the amount of blood she saw. Even if their baby wasn't coming today, she needed to get to the hospital.

With adrenaline pumping and her pulse matching it, Olli turned to leave the bathroom and get dressed. She needed to be ready to go the moment Spur arrived. She had no idea where he was on the ranch, but he rode a horse to work, and that would take him a few minutes to get back even if he'd been working on the far west side of the ranch closest to their house.

Olli went into her master closet and pulled on a pair of her maternity jeans. They were almost too small, and tears sprang to her eyes as she realized today might be the last day she'd wear them.

She tugged her nightgown over her head and let it drop to the floor. Her vision blurry, she simply grabbed whatever T-shirt was closest. She pulled that on and looked at the floor to find shoes. The world spun as she moved her head too fast, and Olli immediately flung her hand out to find something to steady herself.

"Don't let me fall," she prayed, the words just bursting from her mouth. At the same time, Olli knew she was going to fall. She had no balance, and she couldn't find a focus point.

She tipped sideways, stumbling in that direction. But with a nine-months-pregnant belly, Olli could not find her center of gravity. Everything happened so fast, and before she knew it, she'd landed on her hip, and a pain shot down her left leg and up into her back.

She cried out and grunted at the same time, trying to keep her head from hitting the floor. She failed spectacularly at that too, and all in three seconds' time, Olli found herself lying on the floor, halfway in the closet and halfway in the bathroom in front of Spur's sink.

The scent of her candles wafted through her nose, and she took a long, deep breath to try to quiet her fear. Another contraction hit her, and pain filled her whole body.

She screamed, but there was no one to hear. When her voice ran out, her head throbbed from where she'd hit it, and the room continued to spin. She closed her eyes to tame the nausea, but she knew she couldn't stay here.

She also knew she couldn't get up by herself. She'd left her phone on the nightstand, and she still didn't have shoes.

Olli couldn't believe her mind had thought about a stupid pair of shoes. She should be sobbing and begging God to save her baby. Her clothes felt wet in the wrong places, and she tried to roll onto her side unsuccessfully. If she could get herself up, she could grab onto the handle of a drawer in the bathroom vanity and at least attempt to get to her knees.

"Olli!" Spur called, and hope filled her heart.

"In the bathroom," she said, but her voice didn't make it out of the room.

"Olli?" His boots sounded as he jogged down the hall, and then he filled the doorway. "Olli." The last time he said her name, it came out only as air. "No, no." He rushed to her and cradled her head in his lap. "Look at me, Olli."

She tilted her head back and looked at him, noticing the pure panic in his face.

"Talk to me," he demanded. "I'm calling nine-one-one."

"No," Olli said, and that got Spur to realize she wasn't passed out. "We don't have time to wait for the ambulance. Help me up."

"Olli, you're bleeding." His eyes moved down her body. "A lot."

"That's how I know there's no time to wait for the ambulance." Olli tried to push herself up again, and with both of Spur's strong, big hands, she managed to get to her knees. He helped her all the way back to her feet, and she planted both palms against the bathroom counter and cried at the pain in her hip and rolling through her lower back.

"I don't know how to walk," she whimpered.

Spur never moved more than an inch away from her. "I'm calling Blaine. He was just leaving his house, and I told him to stand by." He dialed with one hand, keeping the other on Olli's waist, and he barked into the phone, "I need you here."

He set the phone down on the counter and touched the speaker icon. "Olli fell, and she's bleeding a lot. She doesn't think we have time to wait for the ambulance, and she's not sure she can get to the truck."

"Get our baby bag," Olli said as more clarity entered her mind.

Spur met her eyes in the mirror. "I'm okay," she said.

"Right now. Go get the baby bag. It's on my side of the bed. Then come put your arm around me, and I can do it."

"I'm two minutes away," Blaine said through the phone. "I'm literally turning onto your lane right now."

Spur grabbed his phone and darted back into the bedroom. Olli looked into the mirror and stared into her own eyes. "You can do this," she told herself. "Get to the truck and let your husband get you to the hospital." She was steady enough now to put one hand on her belly instead of using it to balance against the counter. "Hold on, baby. Just hold on a little longer, please."

CHAPTER 5

S pur handed the baby bag to Blaine and did what Olli said he should. He put his arm under one of hers and practically lifted her off the ground. She managed to take small steps that way, and they made slow progress toward the front door, which Blaine had left open.

Together, he and his brother managed to get Olli into the front seat of the truck, which Spur leaned back. Blaine had put a towel on the seat and he said, "I'm calling the hospital now," with his phone to his ear. "So they'll be ready."

Olli groaned with the arrival of another contraction, and Spur hadn't been counting, but she'd had one in the bathroom when he'd re-entered it, and one on the way from the bedroom to the truck. They were coming faster and faster, and he needed to get her to town quickly.

He ran around the front of the truck and got them

going in the right direction. "Talk to me, love," he said. "Tell me something."

"You tell me something," she said back. "I'm too focused on holding the baby in to talk."

Spur could barely watch the road, because all he wanted to do was stare at Olli and make sure she didn't pass out. She would never understand the intensity of the fear and panic that overcame him when he found her down on the ground as he had a few times now. She always insisted she was okay, but Spur honestly couldn't wait for the baby to be born so she could return to some semblance of her normal health.

He'd managed to convince her to go to the doctor after Halloween, once everyone had found out about her falls. There had been nothing on any scan, anywhere, to indicate why she'd fallen down. She'd felt vindicated; perhaps she really had tripped over her shoes.

Spur wasn't so sure, because the vertigo and loss of balance didn't seem right to him, even for someone as pregnant as Olli.

He turned onto the highway and pressed on the accelerator. Blaine would tell everyone in the family about the baby, and before he knew it, Spur would have to go out into the waiting room and tell all the Chappells to quiet the heck down. Some of them—Conrad and Ian especially—could wake the dead, and his stomach tightened.

Olli panted and reached for the door handle, gripping it until her fingers turned white.

"Daddy found a new horse," Spur said, his mind racing. "She's a ten-month old, and she's real pretty, Olls. You'd really like her. Her owner named her Mercury, but Daddy doesn't think it fits. He's been workin' with her and ridin' her to get a better sense of her personality. What do you think we should name her?"

"What color is she?"

"Grayish," he said. "Light gray. Silver. Some white." He glanced at her, and thankfully, her fingers had released the door handle.

"So not Snowdrop." She smiled at Spur, and in moments like these, she was her true self. The woman he'd fallen in love with, and the one who worked harder than anyone he knew. The one with amazing ideas, and all the creativity in the world to take her business to the next level. Her pregnancy had been hard on her in a lot of ways, and Spur's whole heart squeezed for her.

"Not Snowdrop," he said with a chuckle. "We'll find you a Snowdrop, my love." He reached over and took her hand in his, pressing a kiss to her palm. "Daddy's thinking something like Stormcloud or something."

"That's not a racehorse name," Olli said.

"Yeah, but we won't register that until she starts to race," Spur said. "Gotta have something to call 'em in normal life." He moved to go around someone driving much slower than him, and he continued telling Olli about the horse his father had gotten. Every time she had a contraction, he glanced at the clock on the dash.

Before he knew it, they'd arrived at the emergency room, and he jumped from the truck and ran inside. "My wife is in labor," he yelled, and a woman rose from the desk.

He knew Jenna Paine, and she signaled that she'd heard him.

He hurried back outside, where Olli—blast her—had the door open and her legs out. "Wait, wait," he called, and he barred her from getting out any further. "They're coming to help." He put both hands on her knees. "Olli, the contractions are three minutes apart. Please wait for the wheelchair."

"I don't want a wheelchair," she said.

"Too bad." Spur looked at her with a frown between his eyes. "I can't watch you fall again, and I can't find you on the floor, bleeding again."

She met his eyes, and Spur finally thought she got the meaning of what he'd said. "Fine," she said, tears filling her eyes. "This isn't how I wanted this to go."

Spur smiled and tucked her into his chest. "Just think, love. The baby will be born today, and you won't have to be so uncomfortable anymore." He'd loved her so much before she'd gotten pregnant. Watching her deal with the morning sickness and bloated ankles had only cemented her saint-hood in his eyes. She'd done extremely hard things, day after day, hour after hour, to bring his baby into the world.

There was no greater sacrifice, and Spur loved Olli on a whole new level he hadn't even known existed.

"I don't know if I can ever do this again," Olli whispered, clinging to him now. "What if we only get one baby, Spur?"

"Then we get one, baby," he whispered. "One's enough." He stroked her hair, because for him, one child was enough. For the Chappell family, it was inconceivable, but Spur had always done things a little unconventionally. Besides, he had seven brothers, and they could make up the difference in grandchildren.

He knew Olli wanted at least two children, because she didn't think the life of a single child would be very fun. Spur prayed for his wife, that she would be calm and focused, all doubts and worries blocked for now.

"Here we are," a woman said, and Spur released his wife and turned toward her. He backed out of the doorway so they could get the chair closer and help Olli, frowning.

He knew that voice. He knew that woman's face. Her hair was the wrong color though, and she'd aged...

"Katie?" he said, all the lightbulbs in the world hitting him in the brain.

The woman turned toward him, her smile somewhat plastic. She wore the blue-green scrubs nurses did and she said, "Hello, Spur. It's been a while."

"Your hair..." He looked at the blonde pixie cut, and it didn't suit her at all. "How long have you been a nurse?"

Olli groaned, and Spur looked past his ex-wife to his current one, praying for his own focus now. *Thanks for the ironic twist*, he thought wryly.

"Let's get you out, love," he said to Olli once her contraction had passed. "They're coming every three minutes or so. They only last about thirty seconds, as you just saw." He wedged himself into the tiny space between the open door and the wheelchair and lifted his wife right into his arms.

He turned and set her in the chair, his own back protesting the movement. They both grunted, and at least Olli got to ride for the next few minutes. "There you go."

"Thank you, baby." Olli stroked her hand down the side of his face, and then they were off to the races. Or at least the maternity ward.

* * *

Eight exhausting hours later, Spur finally cradled a tiny baby boy in a bunch of warmed blue blankets. He pressed a kiss to his son's forehead, marveling at the papery, waxy texture of his skin. The baby's heartbeat pulsed right there in his head, which was completely void of hair.

Olli had been through a lot of ups and downs to finally bring him into the world, and she'd wept at the very sight of him. Spur understood the feeling, and he looked up as the nurse opened the door.

"I'll be right back, love," he said to Olli. "Take a little nap, okay?" He kissed her too and then followed the nurse into the hallway. He wasn't really sure where the waiting room was, because he'd come up with Olli from the emergency room, and he swore the hospital had back hallways and secret elevators the public didn't know about.

The whole thing was a maze, and it would be a miracle if he could get back to his wife without an escort.

"Right there," the nurse said, indicating the wide open area at the end of the hall. "They're all there."

"Thanks," Spur said, flashing her a smile. He went the

rest of the way alone, having a hard time walking while holding the baby. He wasn't sure if he should look at the infant to make sure he was still breathing or look forward so he didn't fall down or run into someone.

He glanced up to find Cayden standing at the mouth of the hall, and he turned his head to the left. "Here he comes."

A crowd started to gather around Cayden, with Mom right up front. She cried openly, and Spur just smiled at her as he approached. "Here he is," he said, his voice awed and reverent.

"Oh, he's perfect," Mom said, covering her mouth.

"We named him Gus Jeffrey Chappell."

"Gus is so cute," Ginny said, and Spur couldn't believe she and Cayden had interrupted their honeymoon to be here. At the same time, he really could, because Olli and Ginny had been best friends for a couple of decades now, and Spur knew Ginny wanted a baby more than anything.

He passed baby Gus to Mom, and he met Ginny's eye silently communicating to her that she'd get to hold him second.

Free from the baby, Spur rocked back on his heels. "And funny story—Katie was the emergency room nurse who checked us in."

Dozens of eyebrows went up, and Ian asked, "Your ex-wife?"

"Yep." Spur couldn't believe it either, but the interaction hadn't been horrible.

"I didn't know she was a nurse," someone said, and Spur echoed the sentiment. He watched his mother coo at the baby, and everything finally felt like it would be all right.

Daddy took him into a hug, and Spur clung to his father with everything he had. "How's Olli?" Daddy asked.

"Good," Spur said through a rough throat. "She did real good. She's exhausted, and I'm going to try to get her to let the nurses tend to Gus through the night. We'll see."

Daddy stepped back, a glow on his face Spur had never seen before. "You're going to be a great father," he said, and he stepped back over to Mom and ran his rough cowboy fingers across Gus's head. It was sweet to see the tenderness of his touch, as Spur had always known his father to be strong and commanding. He knew how to get a job done, and how to do it right. Spur had learned so much from his dad, and he realized in that moment that it extended beyond just ranch knowledge.

He'd learned how to be a father from his own father, and he hadn't even known it.

Despite the slightly crazy start to the day, when Spur took his son back to Olli and the three of them sat together in the hospital room, he felt a sense of peace and calm that he desperately needed.

"I love you, Olls," he whispered as he let his eyes drift closed.

"Love you too, Spur."

CHAPTER 6

Lisa scrubbed at the carpet in Daddy's office, trying to get the dust lines out. He'd had a half-dozen boxes down there, and Lisa had just finished going through them. Most days, she could work around the house for a few hours before she simply couldn't concentrate.

She'd sorted everything into several piles—stuff for her to keep, stuff to ask Bruce and Kelly about, stuff to donate to Goodwill, stuff to throw away, and stuff to shred.

Daddy was a bit of a packrat, and she'd found old notebooks of his from the early nineties. They had all the names of his studs and who he'd scheduled them to cover. Lisa had put those in the shred pile, because she didn't want his systems out there for anyone to see.

She'd taken over the color-coded notebooks this year, and it had taken her a solid month to even grasp what she was doing. Daddy had a system for how often a stud could be hired out, and he liked doing things geographically, so he wasn't driving all over Kentucky for the entire spring.

Her biceps ached, but she kept scrubbing at the carpet, bringing up the ground-in dust bunnies. Bruce and Kelly hadn't stepped foot in this office yet, and Daddy had been gone for five days. They hadn't been the ones to go through his clothes and sort them. They hadn't been the ones to find Daddy had passed away in the middle of the night.

A wave of sorrow threatened to submerge Lisa and drag her under for miles. She ground her teeth together and slid the vacuum attachment along the baseboard in the closet. Once she got the carpet clean, she'd move the sorted items back inside.

Daddy had said the night before he'd died that the will was done, and Lisa had a meeting with the lawyer that afternoon. She tried to do all of the work around the house and with Daddy's personal items in the morning, because she needed to escape in the afternoons.

Working the farm and taking care of horses wasn't really a chore for her, and she could work outside in the sunshine and find peace again.

Then, the whole cycle started again the next day.

Lisa wasn't sleeping well, because the house was far too quiet now. Daddy never had made much noise, but it was amazing how much energy another body in the house, however quiet, put out. She hated being in the farmhouse alone, but it was better than being there with Mama.

She'd stayed for three nights, and she'd only left yesterday because Lisa had found a letter for her from

Daddy. She'd read it in private, and an hour later, she'd stood on the front porch saying good-bye. Lisa wondered what Daddy had said, but in the end, she didn't care. It had gotten Darla to go back to Georgia, and that was where she belonged.

Lisa sat back on her haunches and sighed, the loud roar of the vacuum filling her ears and blocking out all other noise. She finally reached up and switched it off, the newfound silence twice as loud as the vacuum cleaner had been.

She got to her feet, her back pulling in a bad way. A groan came out of her mouth, but Lisa knew a pain pill and a hot shower would have her good as new.

She had no appetite, but she forced herself to take one of Daddy's protein shakes from the fridge after she'd cleaned up and dressed in her best skirt and blouse. She wore these to church, and she figured she could wear them to meet with the lawyer.

She gripped the steering wheel as she drove to town, and she peered at the sign for Hitchens Law Office for a good minute before she went inside. Her phone chimed as she reached the secretary, and she said, "I have an appointment with Mister Thatcher," as she pulled her phone out of her purse. "Lisa Harvey."

"He'll be out in a minute," the woman said, and Lisa nodded. She moved over to the brown leather couch and perched on the edge of it to read her message. It had come from Duke, and he'd once again offered to come help her that afternoon or evening.

He'd called or texted every day since Daddy's death, and he was the only bright spot in Lisa's life. He brought a smile to Lisa's face, but she still didn't want him to come work at Horses by Harvey. He had plenty of his own work to do around Bluegrass, and Lisa was managing her job just fine.

Daddy employed other cowboys and cowgirls, and even Kelly had stepped in to handle a few phone calls to the payroll company in the past couple of days.

Her usual bitterness when she thought about how much her half-brothers did around the stud farm compared to what she did arrived, and she frowned as she tapped out a response to Duke.

You're so sweet to offer – again – but I'm okay. The farm is okay. She stared at the letters, wondering if he'd stop asking if she denied him every single time. Of course he would. Most men did, and Duke was nothing more than a man. Maybe one of the best-looking men Lisa had ever met, and maybe one of the most capable. But still just a man.

She remembered the way he'd shown up at the hospital even though she'd said she didn't need him there. The truth was, she *had* needed him there. She hadn't turned him away then, and she wouldn't be surprised if he showed up at the farm sooner rather than later.

Lisa didn't want it to be when she couldn't talk to him, or when she'd just gotten out of the shower. It felt wrong to be setting a date with the dark, dreamy cowboy, but she started typing anyway.

I wouldn't say no to your muscles in the office tomorrow morning, though. She added a smiley face to the message and sent it. *I've been going through Daddy's things, and there are quite a few boxes I need moved and loaded into my truck.*

Makin' me work on the weekend, Duke sent back. *I see how you are.* He sent a laughing emoji, and Lisa found herself smiling again. *What time is too early?*

I'm not sleeping well, she admitted to him. *I'll be up when you get here, I'm sure.*

I'll see you tomorrow then.

Lisa nodded to herself and looked up as a man entered the lobby area. "Lisa?" he drawled. "I'm Leon Thatcher." He extended his hand toward her, and Lisa scrambled to her feet to shake it.

"C'mon back," he said, and he wore a pair of black slacks, a white shirt, and a blue tie...with a dark cowboy hat. Daddy wouldn't have trusted a man who didn't wear a cowboy hat.

Lisa followed him down the hall to the office in the back corner, and she knew her half-brothers and their wives had been there that morning. Her nerves hammered at her composure, chipping it away with every breath.

She gathered everything she could control as close as she could, holding it as tightly as she could.

"Please, sit," Leon said, gesturing to a nice pair of leather wingback chairs.

Lisa took the one on the left, as it faced more of the desk. She crossed her legs and tapped to open the voice recorder on her phone. "Can I record this?" she asked, glancing up as Leon's desk chair squeaked.

He sat and swiveled back toward her. "Sure thing, sweetheart."

Lisa painted a false smile on her face, because she hated it when men twenty years older than her called her sweetheart. It felt so condescending.

"Thank you," she drawled anyway, setting her phone on the edge of his desk. She tapped *record* and looked at him expectantly.

"We just finalized the will two days before your father passed away," Leon said. "I think he was really holding on until that was done, because he wanted to make sure you were taken care of."

Lisa didn't know what to say, so she simply nodded.

"Your father has written you a letter, and he wanted me to give it to you after we go over the will and what you'll be entitled to." He placed a simple, plain, white envelope on the desk in front of him, and Lisa wanted to lunge forward and grab it.

She could barely take her eyes from it while he pulled out a folder. "The will is quite simple. Your daddy left the farmhouse to you, free and clear. All you have to do is take his death certificate to the county courthouse and get the title transferred over." He smiled, and relief started to coat over some of the buzzing in Lisa's body.

"Now, your father owns Horses by Harvey." Leon pinned her with those bright blue eyes. "That's seventy-four acres of land, with multiple outbuildings, over a dozen pieces of equipment, a staff of seven, and thirty-one horses, as I'm sure you're aware."

"I am," Lisa said, clearing her throat. "I've been working the farm for two decades. Full time. Part-time before that." Lisa couldn't remember a day when she wasn't toddling after Daddy on the farm, and she literally couldn't imagine what her life would be like if she couldn't keep her job.

"Your father knew you wanted the farm," Leon said. "He had a number of reservations, and in the end, he has split the farm among you, and his two sons, Bruce Baxter and Kelly Kyle." Leon cleared his throat and leaned back in his chair.

Lisa wasn't sure what to make of his body language. He seemed nervous now, and Lisa drew in a breath, trying to get the extra oxygen to calm down her pulse. She felt like she was choking on her heart.

"I'll just read it," Leon said, picking up his glasses and settling them on the end of his nose. "Your father was of sound mind when he made these decisions, and I was in his presence for the whole discussion. I witnessed him signing the documents."

Lisa nodded and uncrossed her legs, almost like she was going to flee before she found out what Daddy had done.

"I, Wayne Wyatt Harvey, leave Horses by Harvey, the entirety of the business, all of the land except where the farmhouse sits and the surrounding lawn and garden that belong to the farmhouse—as those belong to my daughter Lisa Leslie Harvey—all of the buildings, the equipment, vehicles, animals, and assets of the business to my three children as follows."

Leon cleared his throat again and continued. "To Bruce

Baxter Harvey, fifteen percent if he will continue to maintain the buildings. If he chooses not to do so, in whatever way he deems fit, whether that be by performing the maintenance himself or by hiring adequate construction workers, he forfeits his inheritance to Horses by Harvey. He will be given several opportunities to improve his performance if the majority owner isn't happy with the maintenance."

All Lisa could think was *fifteen percent? That's hardly anything.*

Bruce had hardly worked at the stud farm for a while now, though. He'd founded a western wear clothing company, and he spent almost all of his time working on that. Kelly was the CFO of that company, and he spent even less time at the stud farm than Bruce did.

"To Kelly Kyle Harvey, I leave fifteen percent of Horses by Harvey if he will continue to oversee the quarterly financials, as well as the annual financial requirements of the farm. If he chooses not to do so, in whatever way he deems fit, whether that be by performing the maintenance himself or by hiring an adequate financial planner, advisor, or tax specialist, he forfeits his inheritance to Horses by Harvey. He will be given several opportunities to improve his performance if the majority owner isn't happy with the maintenance."

Leon looked up from the papers he held in front of his face. His eyes shone like stars, and he smiled at her. "To my daughter, Lisa Leslie Harvey, I leave the remaining seventy percent of Horses by Harvey if she will commit to reading my personal letter to her and abiding by the advice given therein. In addition, she must allow for proper disciplinary time for her half-brothers to complete their tasks. And finally, she must find a partner to help her with the stud farm that is as committed to it as she is. This partner must be found within six months, and the transfer of Horses by Harvey will not be complete until a marriage certificate is produced to Leon J. Thatcher, who should also attend the wedding."

Lisa's heart zinged around inside her chest. Seventy percent. She was the majority owner of the stud farm.

She needed to read the personal letter right now. She could be kind to her half-brothers.

Her mind seized.

"I have to get married?" she asked.

"Within six months," Leon said, setting the papers on the desk. He wore a sympathetic look.

Lisa opened her mouth to speak, but no words would form.

"He explains in the letter." Leon gave it a finger flick and it slid across the desk. "At least, he said it did. He did not show it to me."

Lisa grabbed the envelope and slid her fingernail under the sealed flap. She needed to know right this second why Daddy thought it was even close to okay to require her to get married in order to keep the farm.

CHAPTER 7

Duke looked toward the front door as loud pounding sounded on it. "Who's that?" Lawrence asked. The two of them sat at the dining room table, where they'd just sat down with grilled cheese sandwiches and bowls of potato chowder their mother had brought by yesterday.

"I don't know. No one knocks on the front door. They just come in."

"I'll get it," Lawrence said when Duke still didn't move. He walked out of the kitchen and into the foyer to open the door. "Oh, howdy, Lisa."

Duke dang near fell as he tried to get up. It happened so fast, and his chair toppled over in his haste. He grabbed a paper towel and wiped his mouth, wishing he had time to run upstairs and brush his teeth.

Why? he asked himself as he strode toward the front door too. *You're not going to kiss her tonight.*

They hadn't even gone out on a single date.

"Lisa?" he asked, trying to see past Lawrence. His brother finally moved out of the way, and the beautiful brunette that had been following him into his dreams stood there. She'd obviously been crying, and she wrung her hands together like she had some very bad news to deliver.

"Heya, honey," he said, stepping right past Lawrence and drawing Lisa to his chest. "What's goin' on? Why are you here?"

Her arms came up and around Duke, holding him as tightly as he held her. He sure liked that, and he didn't even mind that Lawrence hadn't moved more than two feet. Lisa sobbed into his chest, and Duke couldn't imagine what she could've lost this time to make her cry like this.

The farm, he thought.

"Lisa," he said. "Did your daddy get the will done?" He stepped back and gripped her shoulders. "What happened? Are you physically hurt?"

She shook her head and kept her gaze on the floor. "I got the farm," she said, but she sounded absolutely miserable about it.

"That's good, right?" Duke asked. "Are these happy tears?" He knew women cried those, and he sure did hope that was what was happening here. At the same time, he didn't think so. He'd felt the desperation in the way she'd clung to him, and no one sobbed from joy.

She may not have a mark on her physically, but something had hurt her.

"I'll give you some privacy," Lawrence said, and being

the best brother in the world that he was, he returned to the kitchen, picked up his bowl and plate with his sandwich, and went upstairs.

"Come inside," Duke said. "Come eat something. Have you eaten?"

She shook her head, and he noticed a folded envelope in one of her hands.

"What's that?" he asked, threading his fingers through her free hand. "Do you want a sandwich? Soup?"

"I'll take some soup," she said.

Duke set about heating it up for her, and he filled the silence with the happenings of his day. With another bowl of hot chowder, he sat down at the table. "Okay enough to tell me now?"

"Everything is a mess," she said. "Literally and figuratively." She picked up a spoon. "I could work in that farmhouse every day, all day, for months, and I still wouldn't get it cleaned out. No one's helping me, and I still don't know why Bruce and Kelly were so resistant to me taking over the farm."

"You said you got it," Duke said, spooning up some chowder.

"Yes." Lisa nodded, her dark hair spilling over her shoulders and covering the pretty white blouse with pink flowers that she wore. She also had on a black pencil skirt and heels, and Duke liked this sexy, chic, church look as much as her cowgirl boots and dirty jeans.

"But it comes with conditions," she said. "I have to work with my half-brothers. They both got fifteen percent, and I got seventy. Bruce maintains all of our buildings right now. Well, he has a company do it, but it's the same thing. He has to keep doing that. Kelly double-checks all the financials; he pays our quarterly taxes; does an annual review, and files all the business taxes. He has to keep doing that."

"Okay," Duke said. "And you got the rest." He offered her a smile. "That's great, honey."

She didn't look like it was great. In fact, she gave him a glare and took a bite of her soup. After swallowing, she said, "It would be great if that was it. It's not."

"What else?" he asked.

She cleared her throat and shook her hair back over her shoulders. "Daddy wrote me a personal letter. I read it, and I freaked out, and I ran out of the lawyer's office." Tears gathered in her eyes. She shook her head. "I've just been driving around and around, and I don't know. I just ended up here."

She gave him a watery smile, sniffed, and wiped her face. "I'm such a mess." She tilted her head back. "Lord, why am I such a mess?"

"Hey," Duke said. "You're not a mess." He covered her hand with his. "At the risk of you freaking out, what's in the letter?"

Lisa closed her eyes in a long blink and then picked up the folded envelope she'd discarded on her right side. She opened her eyes and unfolded the paper.

"My dearest Lisa." She paused, her chin quivering. "I can't read it again. You read it." She thrust the single sheet of paper toward him, and Duke hastened to set down his spoon and take the page.

His eyes scanned ahead, but he had trouble latching onto any key words. He went back to the top and started again.

My dearest Lisa. My daughter. The light in my whole world. I love you forever, and I want the very best for you.

I know you think that's Horses by Harvey, and maybe it is. I want you to be really sure, though, and I want you to know there is no shame, regret, or worries about walking away from the stud farm if it's not what you want. I will not be upset or angry. Heck, I won't even be here.

Duke paused and smiled, because that last part was true. A man could work his entire life and accumulate all the wealth in the world. None of it mattered, because even the richest, most powerful man or woman on Earth couldn't take what they'd amassed here on this planet with them.

Not Wayne Harvey. No one.

I lost my first wife to a terrible accident, and I didn't think I could find love again. I did, though, and then I lost your mama to the stud farm. Lisa, when you own the farm, you're married to it. It can consume a person, and not in a good way.

I know you're willing to be consumed in such a way, and I admire that. I was too. I was always all-in with the stud farm. I left the majority of it to you, because I know you are too. But I don't want that for you. I want more.

I want you to have your own dreams too, and I know those include a husband and family. I also know the thought of those two things scares you senseless. I would advise you to find a way to believe in love and marriage. I know I've failed in showing you that two people can find love and stay married, but Lisa, look around. Plenty of people do it.

I want you to have the farm. I want you to pass it to your son or daughter. In order to do that, you need a husband. He needs to be as committed to the stud farm—and you—as you are. If he is, you two will have the happiest ever-after known to mankind.

I know you'll be upset and confused about the marriage requirement, but I have to do it, Lisa. If you want the farm, you have to do it. You have to find a way to break down all those walls and let someone in. Really let someone in.

Your mom couldn't do that, and it took me a while to figure out how too.

I believe in you. I trust Horses by Harvey to you, because I know you're the one person who loves it as much as I do. I just want you to find a human being to love that way too.

Forgive me if you can. I love you.

Daddy

Duke let the paper settle back to the table, his mind running in ten different directions. "Wow," he finally managed to say. "I see why you freaked out and ran away."

"I have to get married in order to keep the farm," she said as if she hadn't quite put the words in the right order until then. "I have six months to do it."

Duke looked at her, the answer right in front of him. He needed to talk to Trey and Beth, because they'd gotten married before they were actually in love. They'd needed to tie the knot so Beth could enter her horse in the Sweetheart Classic, and Trey had said he'd do it.

Could Duke marry Lisa so she could keep her stud farm?

That and at least a dozen other questions zipped from one side of his brain to the other, rendering him mute for now. He wasn't even sure how he could keep breathing for how much mental energy it took to simply think.

Lisa gathered up the letter and stuffed it back into the envelope. "You're doing what I did," she said. "Sitting there, staring, trying to comprehend."

"It's a bit of a shock," Duke admitted. "Good thing Lawrence went upstairs."

Lisa dipped her spoon into her soup and looked up at him. "Yeah? Why's that?"

Duke shifted in his seat. "Well, aren't you going to ask me to marry you?"

CHAPTER 8

The grin on Duke's face added some radiance to the room. Lisa's first reaction was to scoff and tell him no. Of course she wasn't going to ask him to marry her. She had plenty of other choices, and all of them were better than him.

That would be lying, though, and Lisa didn't need to add that to the things conspiring against her.

"Stop smiling like that," she said, annoyed at him. She reminded herself that she and Duke barely got along, and a marriage between the two of them would likely be the most toxic thing on the planet.

"How should I be smiling?" Duke asked, his dark eyes moving to the food in front of him. She wished he wasn't wearing such a perfect shirt, all that brown, black, and white woven together into a sophisticated plaid pattern. He picked up his grilled cheese sandwich and took a bite.

With horror, she realized she'd let him read the whole

letter, along with all the parts about how she had walls up and how she needed to learn to let people in. Everything Daddy had said in the letter was true, but that didn't mean she wanted the world to read it.

"I came here for help," she said, sliding the envelope under her thigh. She didn't have pockets in this skirt, and it pressed against her knees on both sides when she sat.

"Yeah, and askin' me to marry you would help."

"Why don't *you* ask *me* to marry you?" she shot at him.

Duke's face blanked, and that was all the answer Lisa needed. "Exactly." She pointed her spoon at him before going in for another bite. "Did you make this?"

"Mom," he said. "She keeps us decently fed here when Cayden's gone." Duke finished his sandwich and stood up. "Tell you what, I can't wait for Ginny to move in. She's a good cook."

"Are you going to stay living here?" Lisa asked, glad they weren't talking about getting married anymore, though that was all she really needed to talk about.

"Yeah, for a while," Duke said. "They said they didn't mind. Lawrence will get married in the spring, and I don't know. Something will happen with me."

"Yeah, something," Lisa murmured, looking out the window to the darkness beyond it. She didn't know how anyone could keep their blinds open at night like this. She hated the way it made her feel like someone was watching her, as their eyes had adjusted to the dim light, but hers hadn't.

She pulled her gaze from the scary world outside that she

couldn't see, thinking it to be very much like looking into the future. It was wide open, with any number of possibilities. She couldn't see what it held, and that scared her more than anything.

More than allowing someone in?

She glanced at Duke as he returned to the table. "We've got ice cream," he said. "If you want some when you finish that."

Lisa nodded as she took another bite of soup. "I like ice cream."

"Who doesn't like ice cream?" Duke asked, his smile infectious.

Lisa returned it. "Actually, one of my sisters-in-law is lactose intolerant. She doesn't like ice cream."

"Yes, she does," Duke said. "She just can't eat it. There's a difference."

Lisa watched him settle back into his seat and fold his arms, grinning like he'd just dropped the best punch line ever. "How long have you been waiting to use that line?" she asked.

Duke burst out laughing, and that caused joy to course through her.

Lisa finished her soup, and Duke kept the conversation light. The moment a pause entered the room, she looked at him.

Big mistake, her mind screamed.

"So." Duke got up and went into the kitchen. He opened the freezer, and then a drawer. "What are you going to do? Who's going to be the lucky groom?"

"I don't know." Lisa ran her hands up her face and into her hair. She scratched her nails along her scalp and raked them through her hair.

Duke set a couple of bowls on the table, along with more spoons. The ice cream came next, and he brought three choices with him: maple nut, blackberry cheesecake, and mint chocolate chip.

"What's your poison?" he asked.

"Mint chocolate chip."

"You got it, honey."

Lisa watched him peel off the lid and dig into the hard ice cream. "Do you call everyone honey?"

He glanced her way, something edgy in his eyes. "Not everyone," he said.

"But more than me."

"No," he said, sliding a bowl with four scoops of ice cream in front of her. There was no way she could eat all of that, and she told him so.

"Then don't," he said. "I don't care."

She didn't want to fight with Duke Chappell. The fact that she'd driven around Dreamsville and Lexington for hours and then shown up at Bluegrass Ranch—crying, no less—meant something.

What, Lisa was still trying to figure out.

She erred again by meeting Duke's gaze once more, and she'd lost several seconds while he'd scooped himself some blackberry cheesecake ice cream.

She opened her mouth to fill it with mint chocolate

chip, but she blurted out, "I want you to be the lucky groom."

Her eyes widened, and a squeak came out of her mouth. She slapped one hand over it and stared at him.

A slow, delicious smile curved Duke's mouth. "How about we start with a first date? Tomorrow night?"

* * *

Duke Chappell knew how to date a woman. He knew how to dress up nice, open doors, and say all the perfectly charming cowboy things, in that perfectly charming cowboy voice of his.

Lisa felt like a queen, and they'd only just put in their drink orders. She looked at him across the table, and she wondered if he'd somehow gotten ahold of her diary so he'd know that her favorite color was blue, and that she liked it when men wore a white cowboy hat with a bright periwinkle shirt.

His jeans had appeared brand new, and everything about him—from the belt buckle to the polish on his cowboy boots—was pristine. She was definitely attracted to him the way the sun kept the planets in orbit.

"Have you dated a lot lately?" Duke asked, reaching for a piece of bread.

Lisa nearly choked, but she hadn't put anything in her mouth yet. She shook her head. "You?"

"Here and there," he said. "I think my brothers think I date a lot." He gave her a smile that held some trepidation along the edges. "I guess I go out a lot. No one really captures my attention, though."

Lisa's heart started to flop sideways with every beat. "Is that right?"

"You do, though," he said, smiling more fully as he buttered his bread. "That's okay to say, right?" He took a bite of his bread and looked straight at her, seemingly unembarrassed about what he'd just said.

She swallowed, because if she married this man, she had a feeling he'd be saying a lot of things she'd need to figure out and react to. "Yes," she said slowly, the same way a new warmth had started to spread through her. "That's okay to say."

Duke nodded and finished his bite of bread. "Let's talk about this wedding idea."

Lisa looked away, wishing a waiter or someone would come interrupt them. Better yet, maybe the restaurant would catch on fire and they'd have to evacuate. She reminded herself that she *needed* to talk about the insane wedding proposal she'd blurted out last night.

She thought of the way he'd held her hand at the front door and swept a kiss along her cheek. He'd been nothing but a perfect Southern gentleman, and Lisa had to admit that he had captured her attention completely too. How, she wasn't even sure.

She brought her eyes back to his. "You capture my attention too," she said through a thick throat. "I'm not sure how or why, as you've kind of always rubbed me the wrong way.

And then one day, I don't know, a few months ago, I started to...see you differently."

He started nodding about halfway through her mini speech. "I know exactly what you mean," he said.

"Now there's this thing I have to do," she said. "I'm not sure why, but you were the first person I wanted to tell, because well, I actually did think you could help me solve the problem." She ducked her head. "The more I think about it, the crazier it is. I could hardly sleep last night, and I don't know. Maybe we can just do this the normal way. Go out. See if the attraction grows into something more." She lifted one shoulder, a chill coming over her skin.

"Yeah," he said slowly. He leaned forward and dusted his fingers on his napkin. "But Lisa, what if it doesn't? Then you've wasted all this time on me. Do you even have another prospect for a husband?" He glanced left and right. "Real or fake?"

She shook her head, desperation reaching into her chest and squeezing her heart. "No," she whispered.

His eyes burned with intensity. "I realize you're not well-acquainted with my mother, but I am. If we try to play this as real all the way to a wedding, there's no way it's getting done within your six-month timeframe."

"No?"

"No." He shook his head. "Even if we date for say a month. We decide we're in love. I have to propose. I have to announce it to my family. Mom will go nuts, and she'll want to plan it— she's planned a couple of my brothers' weddings. Since your mama isn't around, mine will literally glom onto you and try to give you the best wedding in the world." He grinned at the end of his sentence, and Lisa couldn't suppress her smile.

"It's a bad idea, trust me." Duke reached for his glass of water, and their conversation got interrupted when the waiter returned with the drinks. Lisa busied herself with unwrapping her straw and squeezing her lemon into her raspberry lemonade. They put in their orders, and once they were alone again, Duke said, "I think... Gosh, I can't believe I'm going to say this." He cleared his throat and didn't speak.

Lisa's adrenaline picked up speed, but she kept her prompt and questions silent.

Duke reached up and took off his cowboy hat, ran his fingers through his thick hair, and put himself back together. Lisa thought about what all that dark hair would feel like between her fingers, and her eyes dropped from the hat to his mouth.

Kissing him would be like touching fire to her lips, she knew that.

Everything inside her grew hot in less time than it took to breathe, and she looked away from him. That seemed to give him the space he needed to speak, because he said, "I think I could fall in love with you," in a real quiet voice. "I already admire so much about you, and I think you're the most stunning woman I've had the pleasure of goin' out with in a long time. But I don't think we have time to do it the quote-unquote *normal* way."

When she looked at him again, Duke had his face tipped

down so she could only see his cowboy hat and his collar. Typical cowboy, and Lisa wished she could wear her cowgirl hat twenty-four-seven so she could hide behind it when she needed to.

He cleared his throat again, reached for his soda glass, and took a drink. His eyes moved all around her, over her shoulder, to his right and left, and then finally landed on hers. "The real question, Lise, is whether you think you can fall in love with me. I don't need an answer right now. There is time to think about this part of it. I just happen to think that if we're going to do this, there has to be the possibility that we can, I don't know." He sighed, the sound full of frustration.

He drew in another deep breath. "I think I need to know that there's the possibility that we could date while we're married. Learn about each other, and have our fights, and do all those things couples do while they're dating and falling in love. Then, eventually, the marriage would be real. If there's not even that possibility, I'm not sure I'm your man."

Lisa couldn't imagine asking anyone else to do this for her. She couldn't even believe she'd asked Duke.

"I didn't know you were so romantic," she said, her voice sounding like it belonged to someone else.

"I didn't either," he said. "I don't really want to deal with my family and explaining everything to them if we split up down the road. Then I'll never hear the end of how I rushed into marriage because I didn't want to be left behind." He shook his head and said, "Never mind. That's not what's important here."

Lisa suspected there was something important there, and he'd only touched on it. She wanted to ask him why he felt left behind, but she held the question for another time. "What is important here?" she asked.

"We can talk about rules and boundaries and all of that if we decide to move forward with this," he said. "I think right now, we both have to decide if there is the real possibility of truly falling in love."

"I don't know how to do that," Lisa said. "Do people just *know* when they meet that special someone?" She searched his face, trying to find the answer.

"I think it feels different, yes," he said.

"That's because you go out a lot," she said, her stomach churning with nervous energy.

"Like I said, you don't have to decide tonight. I think there's time for that. Take a week. Or two. We can go out a few more times. You can see how you feel."

Lisa hated examining her feelings. She'd rather just go through a box of papers in the office or go move a horse from one stable to the other. No feelings required.

She nodded, though, because Duke was right. If there was no possibility of a marriage with him ever being real, she shouldn't put either of them through such a thing. It was legal, and binding, and she needed a few more days to think everything through.

"Okay," Duke said with a big exhale following it. "Tell me what you'd eat for your last meal." He grinned at her, and how he could lighten the mood and make everything normal and comfortable again with a single sentence baffled Lisa.

It also intrigued her and endeared him to her, and she wondered if she did just know that he was someone special and she shouldn't let him get away.

CHAPTER 9

Duke grabbed his toast and dropped it on the counter. The radio played in the homestead, and he liked that he came downstairs to the familiar sound of country music. Sometimes the countryside could be really quiet, and sometimes Duke couldn't handle the silence as it wove through his body, slowly driving him crazy.

He buttered his toast and picked up a piece to take a bite. With the buttery, warm, crunchy bread in his mouth, he grabbed his to-go mug of coffee and headed for the garage exit. He didn't bother to turn off the radio, because Lawrence didn't mind it either, and his brother would be down in a few minutes.

Duke wanted to avoid him for now, because he didn't have a proper explanation for his date with Lisa the previous night, nor did he want to tell Lawrence where he was headed this morning.

His heart sank as he left the garage to the sight of Conrad pulling up in his dark gray truck. He parked behind Duke's truck, which meant he'd have to talk to his next-oldest brother before he left.

Duke and Conrad were only fifteen months apart, and Duke didn't have a childhood memory without Conrad in it. They were alike in so many ways, and yet unique too.

"Mornin'," Conrad said as he got out of the truck. Where Duke had some of the darkest hair and eyes and features in the Chappell family, Conrad had the lighter ones. He definitely had more red in his hair from Mom, and he was more lanky and limbs than bulky and biceps like Duke was.

"Howdy," Duke said, stuffing the rest of his toast in his mouth. He held up his keys, and nodded to Conrad's truck.

"Where you off to?" Conrad asked, turning to go back to his door. He wouldn't have his keys with him, as he left them in the ignition almost all the time.

"Gotta go help at a stud farm," he said.

"The Harveys place?" Conrad asked, interest sparking in his eyes.

"Yep." Duke lifted his coffee travel mug to his lips and sipped. "The funeral is on Monday."

"Right," Conrad said. "You're going?"

"Of course I'm going," Duke said. He'd go whether he'd started having soft and billowy feelings for Lisa or not. "I've known Wayne Harvey for a decade. The man came to Blue-grass every single year."

Conrad nodded, his mouth pursing. "Should we all go?"

"I can't decide that for you," Duke said. "I know Mom and Daddy are going. Spur is too. Not sure about Olli, because she just had the baby, but I think Blaine will be there too." His older brothers helped during covering season a lot with the actual physical work it took to get the mares and the studs in the same barn together.

So much of their business was run on the breeding aspect of their racehorses, and Duke thought all of the Chappells should plan to attend the funeral. He didn't tell Conrad that, though. Conrad and Ian focused on the actual training of their runners, so they weren't as familiar with the stud farms the way Duke was.

"Heard you went out last night," Conrad said, stepping up onto the runners of his truck. He didn't duck down inside the cab to get behind the wheel. Instead, he just peered down at Duke, who stood on the opposite side of the vehicle.

"Yeah." It wasn't unusual for Duke to go out with a woman. It also wasn't that unusual for him to keep quiet about it.

"Even I only get 'yeah'?" Conrad asked, grinning. "You must like this one."

"You know what?" Duke asked, looking up at his brother. "I *do* like this one. A lot. So I don't really want to talk about it yet."

"Fair enough." Conrad sank into his seat, fired up the engine, and pulled his truck into the empty spot on the far right of the driveway.

"Thanks," Duke called to him as he rounded the hood of his truck.

"Wait," Conrad called, and he came jogging over to Duke's vehicle. He wore a worried look with his heavy winter jacket and jeans. "How do you...?" He cleared his throat and looked toward the front door of the homestead. "I need to get past Hilde."

Duke heard what he was really saying. "I would agree with that," he said slowly. "It's been a while since she broke up with you."

"We've been back together and then broken up again three times since Spur's wedding," Conrad said. He focused on the ground now, clearly embarrassed. "I need to get over her. I just don't know how." He glanced at Duke. "How'd you get over Allison?"

"First," Duke said, clapping his hand on Conrad's shoulder. "My relationship with Allison wasn't nearly as serious as yours was with Hilde. They're not the same at all. Second, if you want to move past a woman, especially one who's no good for you, you have to go out with someone else. A lot of someone else's. Two different ones in the same day."

Conrad smiled, but he rolled his eyes too. "Ian would kill me."

"Ian has his own demons to face," Duke said. "You can't let him influence what you do. You're not him." Duke and Conrad had always dated the most out of the brothers, but since Duke had moved out of the ranch house where he'd once lived with Lawrence, Conrad, and Ian, he'd felt freer. Ian possessed some level of toxicity about dating, and it definitely rubbed off on those around him, whether he meant it to or not.

"I know," Conrad said. "I live with him, Duke. We train together all day. Life would be unbearable if he didn't talk to me."

"Then come live in the homestead," Duke said, dropping his hand. He was going to be late to Lisa's, but he told himself helping her clean out her father's office wasn't a date.

"I can't do that," Conrad said. "I'm surprised you're still there."

"Yes, well, things change all the time," Duke said. "I'll see you later." He got behind the wheel of his truck and rolled down his window. "Conrad?"

His brother turned from the mouth of the garage. "Yeah?"

"Ask Abby to dinner."

Surprise crossed Conrad's face, and he wasn't so far away that Duke couldn't see the surprise. It melted from his face as acceptance took over, and Conrad finally nodded and smiled. "Good idea."

"Text me when you get the job done," Duke said, and he chuckled as he rolled up his window. When he was fifteen years old, he'd wanted to ask Sarah Elizabeth to the Homecoming dance. He'd been nervous, because he'd been a sophomore and she was a junior. He'd never really asked a girl out before, and Conrad had said he'd ask Pauline Francis. They'd sat down to breakfast, and while Mom put copious amounts of scrambled eggs and sausage on their plates, they'd agreed to "get the job done" that day and return and report how it had gone.

Since then, they'd been asking women to dinner and dances at a steady clip, always getting the job done.

Duke drove the distance from Bluegrass to the Harvey's farm, taking the quiet, loopy back roads of Kentucky that reminded him how very much he liked living among white fences, sprawling homesteads, and horses with their heads bent in the pastures.

Right now, the grass wasn't particularly green, but it would get back to emerald status come April, and Duke loved springtime in Kentucky more than any other time.

His tires crunched over the gravel leading down to the Harvey house, and he noticed how the driveway didn't hold any extra cars. The garage sat closed, and he parked near it before getting out.

Drawing in a deep breath, he finally allowed himself to think about the conversations he and Lisa had had about getting married. He let himself remember how it felt to hold her hand, and his pulse sped up. He thought about the smooth quality of her skin beneath his lips, and he fantasized about kissing her fully on the mouth, not just quickly brushing his lips along her cheek.

Pure fire burned through him, and Duke couldn't remember the last woman he'd felt this strongly for. Maybe Allison, but he honestly wasn't sure.

He did know he wanted to take Lisa out on another date soon. Tonight, if he could. Tomorrow too. If they were going to convince anyone that they'd fallen madly in love in only a few weeks, they'd need to see each other every single day. Duke wasn't going to complain about that, and he'd fallen so far into his thoughts that he had to blink his way back to the present moment.

"Are you going to come in?" Lisa asked, and he switched his gaze to the front porch. She stood in the corner of it closest to him, leaning against the railing in a bright purple T-shirt, no coat. "You've been standing there for a minute."

"Yeah," he said. "I'm going to come in." He grinned at her and almost went into the snow on the lawn to get to her quicker. Instead, he minded his manners and took the walk down the driveway to the cleared sidewalk and then up to the porch steps.

She met him at the top of the porch, her hand landing on his chest as if she'd touched him there a thousand times before. "We're working inside. I hope you didn't wear outside clothes under this heavy coat."

"Just a T-shirt," he said, her touch radiating through him from the origin point on his chest.

Their eyes met, and Duke wasn't sure what she was thinking. She looked a tiny bit anxious, and Duke was a whole lot nervous. "Dinner tonight?" he asked. "Or I could take you to lunch after we work this morning."

"Either is fine," she said, her eyes dropping to his mouth. Duke took the opportunity to look at her lips too, and she'd slicked something glossy and pink on them. He wanted to know if it was strawberry or cherry or something else entirely.

"Have we decided to do this marriage thing?" she asked, putting her other hand next to the first on his chest.

"I don't know," he said, his throat full of the gravel he'd driven over to get here. "Did we? I thought we were going to take a day or a week to decide if it could be real."

"And we have to talk about rules."

"Mm." He could barely think with her hands on his body, and he was wearing a thick coat, so she wasn't even touching his skin. She stood near though, and the winter wind kicked up, bringing the scent of lemons and peppermint from her hair toward Duke.

"I have one of those," she said. "If we do decide to get married."

"Yeah?" Duke wanted to go inside, as the tips of his ears were starting to freeze. He couldn't move a muscle, though.

Those eyes moved to his mouth again. "Yeah. I don't want our first kiss to be on our wedding day." She looked up and into his eyes, taking a tiny step closer to him.

Duke's natural reaction to her nearness was to take her into his arms, and he did exactly that. Holding her on the front porch of her house sent satisfaction through him, and all of his nervousness evaporated right up into the sky.

"It won't be," he promised.

Lisa ran her fingers up the side of his face, and her touch was cool and comforting at the same time. "Would you kiss me right now, Duke?"

He wasn't going to say no to that, not when she'd asked so nicely, pressed herself so tightly into his chest, and touched him so intimately. He let his eyes drift closed as he leaned down, and while Duke had kissed plenty of women in his thirty-two years of life, he'd never kissed anyone like Lisa Harvey.

Just as he'd predicted, heat engulfed his body. He brought her closer as the kiss quickly turned from peck to passionate.

In that moment, he knew he could fall in love with this woman if given enough time and opportunity, and he could only hope she felt the same. If she did, he'd marry her so she could keep her farm, and they'd figure out how to build the relationship Duke had always dreamed of having.

CHAPTER 10

Lisa had awakened that morning with the idea of kissing Duke in her head. She hadn't been able to get it out, no matter what she'd done. She'd worked for three hours in the pre-dawn light, getting her normal morning chores done before the sun woke the day.

She couldn't sleep anyway, and the list of things to get done that day was endless.

At the very least, she could now cross off *Experience the best kiss of your life*, as Duke continued to kiss her like he cherished her right to her very core.

She finally had the good sense to pull away when she shivered. Despite the heat running through her body, the winter temperatures weren't made for standing outside, kissing handsome cowboys.

Duke wrapped her in his arms, and she curled her arms in front of her to keep them warm. He exhaled slowly, and

Lisa kept her eyes closed as she ducked her head and tucked herself against him.

She hadn't kissed a man in a long, long time, and something had stirred inside her that hadn't been touched in ages. She honestly didn't know what it was, because Lisa was so used to lacing everything tight behind leather cords.

"Should we go in?" he asked when she shivered again, and Lisa stepped out of his arms.

"Sure." She stepped away from him without looking at him and moved over to the door. She opened it, the familiar scent of coffee and bacon meeting her nose. "Daddy made coffee every morning," she said. "I barely drink the stuff, but I keep making it." She led Duke into the kitchen and got down a plate. "Have you eaten?"

"I can eat," he said, and Lisa wasn't sure if that was a yes or a no.

"It's just bacon and eggs," she said, flashing him a smile without really looking at him. "Daddy ate bacon and eggs every day he could."

Duke offered her a warm smile in return, but Lisa spun away from him as her emotions threatened to erupt from her. Her mind whirred as she pinched a few pieces of bacon between the arms on a pair of tongs.

She'd just kissed the man, and now she couldn't look at him. Was that normal? Maybe she shouldn't have kissed him. Maybe she should've waited until he'd brought her home from their second romantic date.

She scooped some eggs onto a plate and spun back to the

island only to find Duke had moved into the space she was trying to occupy. "Oops." The plate hit his chest; the eggs went flying. Lisa couldn't keep her grip on the plate and it clattered to the floor, where it shattered.

"Gol darn it," Duke said. "I'm sorry." He backed up a few steps and immediately bent to retrieve the broken pieces. "I thought you'd hear me walk over. Sorry, Lise."

"It's fine." She crouched to start scooping up the eggs too. "I was sort of...lost for a minute." Her voice broke on the last word, and Duke abandoned his quest to get all the larger pieces of the plate.

"Hey, come here." He stood up and drew her to her full height by taking her hands in his. "It's okay to cry with me, Lisa. I'm the safest place for you right now." He cradled her face in his hands and gave her the sweetest, smallest smile she'd ever seen. "You get to be you when you're with me."

That broke Lisa, and she dissolved into tears. Duke wiped them gently for a moment before folding her back into the safe embrace of his arms.

"You don't have to do this alone, honey," he whispered. "I'm safe, and you can tell me anything. You can cry for no reason. It's safe here."

Lisa needed safety more than anything, and she wondered how Duke had known precisely the right word to use to soothe her soul.

He held her tight until she started to calm, and then he stroked her hair until she stepped away from him.

"I'm sorry," she said, her boot coming down on a piece

of ceramic and crushing it. A new sob ran through her. "Everything is such a mess."

"You don't need to apologize to me," he said. "Have you eaten?"

She shook her head, and the next thing she knew, Duke had scooped her right into his arms. "Oh," she yelped, flailing to put her arms around his neck to hold on. He walked her over to the couch and set her down.

He crouched in front of her, something blazing and earnest in his eyes. "You sit right here, Miss Harvey. I'll get you some breakfast and clean up the kitchen." He grinned, his fingers in hers tightening. "Things are a little bit messy right now, Lisa, but it's nothing we can't fix, okay?"

She nodded, because he was such an enigma to her. He was kind and caring, handsome and hot, the best kisser she'd ever met, and oh-so-calm. She marveled at him, because she'd seen him run toward a horse and catapult into the saddle too, wrestle with an angry mare, and study that notebook of his, a cute little frown line between his eyes.

Of course, she'd never thought it was cute before. Annoying, sure. But now, she found everything about Duke to be attractive and perfect.

"Okay." Duke stood, then leaned down and kissed her again, right on the mouth, before going back into the kitchen. He hummed to himself as he put together a plate of food for her, and not thirty seconds later, he returned with bacon, eggs, and coffee. He set it all on the small table next to the couch and handed her a fork. "Just relax for a minute. I'll have everything cleaned up lickety-split."

He went back into the kitchen, and Lisa did exactly what he'd suggested. She ate as she watched a couple of pheasants through the window. She liked the way the birds walked, and she wished the wild turkey herd that sometimes visited the farm in the winter would make an appearance. There was nothing that made her smile wider than the way the wild turkeys walked, especially if they were moving slowly. Their necks seemed to be like a teeter-totter from their bodies, thrusting forward while the body stayed still, and then the bulk of the bird would catch up to the neck.

She'd finished breakfast and was nursing her coffee when the front door opened. Surprised, she turned that way. She got to her feet quickly when she realized Bruce had arrived unannounced.

"Bruce," she said, casting a quick glance into the kitchen. Duke wasn't there, and Lisa had no idea where he'd gone. "What are you doing here?"

"I figured you'd have had some time to process Daddy's will," he said, stopping just inside the back half of the house where all the living areas were. "Thought maybe we could talk about it." He scanned the area, and Lisa simply watched him.

She'd grown up with Bruce and Kelly as older brothers, and they'd never made her feel like she didn't belong to them until the past year or so.

"Smells like Daddy here," he said, his voice touched with sadness. His eyes came back to Lisa's, and he gave a jerk of his head toward the front door behind him. "There's a truck here. Whose is it?"

"Duke's here," she said, refusing to bring her hands together and let them start to weave around one another. She'd done that since childhood whenever something made her nervous. "He must've stepped into the bathroom or something. I wasn't paying attention."

Bruce's jaw tightened. "Are you two seeing each other?"

"Yes," Lisa said, finally admitting it. If the scorching kiss she'd shared with him on the front porch had told her anything, it was that she could quite possibly marry Duke Chappell and fall madly in love with him. She might as well start telling people they were dating. Then the quickie marriage wouldn't come from out of absolutely nowhere.

People would simply speculate about why they needed to tie the knot so fast. In a town as small as Dreamsville, rumors would fly, but Lisa didn't care. She'd been dealing with rumors and whispers behind her back for years.

"Darla is gone?" Bruce asked, his dark eyes turning hard.

"Yes," Lisa said with a sigh as she sank back onto the couch. "Praise the Lord." She looked down at her hands in her lap, another round of surprise moving through her when Bruce started to chuckle.

He moved to sit on the loveseat opposite her, and she smiled as he kept laughing. Their eyes met, and so much existed between them. She could see the fiercely overprotective older brother who'd come to pick her up from school after Tommy Madsen had cut off her braid. She'd only been eight years old, and Bruce had been twenty. He'd come roaring into the principal's office, demanding to see Dr. Pratt and then her classroom teacher. He'd never once released the frown on his face, and he said Daddy would be pursuing legal action if Tommy wasn't suspended.

He was, and in the end, nothing else had happened. Bruce had taken Lisa to the salon, and he'd made sure she got a haircut that didn't make her look like a boy. She'd loved him so fiercely for that, and as the moment lengthened, Lisa could relate a hundred more stories like that one.

"Will you tell me what changed between us a year ago?" she asked.

Bruce's eyes grew wide, his laughter completely gone now. "You don't know?"

"No." She watched him for any signs, anything that would let her know what she'd done or what she should know.

"Daddy didn't tell you." He said the words in a voice covered in shock as he slouched back into the loveseat. "No wonder you've never said anything."

"What was he supposed to tell me?"

"Did you know you've got a colony of skunks living under your back deck?"

Lisa got to her feet to find Duke coming toward her. "I dang near got sprayed by a small one." He grinned and chuckled. "We need to get them out of there, because they were none too happy about me poking at them with a stick. Oh." He came to a stop, his eyes moving past Lisa to Bruce. "Howdy, Bruce."

Duke recovered quickly, got himself moving again, and shook Bruce's hand. He looked between Lisa and Bruce before stepping over to her and taking her hand in his. "You okay?"

"Fine," she murmured.

He pushed her hair back off her face. "I just took the trash out. I heard something going on under the deck and started to investigate."

"I can call Palmyra," she said. "He comes and takes care of all of our critter problems. He built the fence around the chicken coops to keep the foxes out."

"Perfect," Duke said. "I'll tell ya, I don't want to ever be sprayed by a skunk again. Nasty things." He laughed, and Lisa sure did like the sound of it in this house. These walls hadn't heard such joyous laughter for many long months.

They turned toward Bruce, who still stood in front of the love seat, watching them. She wondered what he saw when he looked at her and Duke together, but she wasn't going to ask that. "Bruce was just going to tell me a juicy, family secret," she said, sitting back on the couch. She tugged on Duke's hand so he'd sit too.

He did, his nerves clear as he brushed something invisible from his T-shirt.

Bruce cleared his throat, but he sat too. "You want him to hear?"

Lisa looked from Bruce to Duke and back. "I think he can," she said. "Bruce, Duke and I are probably going to get married." The words stuck down deep in her chest, and she coughed to clear them out. "You know, to fulfill Daddy's requirement of the will."

Bruce sucked in a breath as surprise rolled across his face.

It only lasted a moment, and then he shuttered it behind resignation. "You know Kelly and I don't really want the stud farm," he said.

"Seems odd," Duke said. "You've been fighting with her about it for months."

Lisa didn't need him to fight her battles for her, but it sure felt nice to have someone in her corner. She squeezed his hand and met his eye when he looked at her. This time, she was the calm one while he wore a thunderstorm in his dark eyes. She shook her head slightly, and he erased the frown from his forehead.

"I apologize," he said. "It's not my place to say anything." He lifted Lisa's hand to his lips and pressed a kiss to the back of her palm. "I'm just on her side, that's all."

"There aren't any sides," Bruce said with a sigh. He suddenly looked all forty-seven of his years, the bags under his eyes a sign that he hadn't been sleeping very well either.

"You were going to tell me something," Lisa said.

Bruce switched his gaze back to her. He and Kelly both had Daddy's dark eyes, but their mother had been blonde, and they both had sandy, mousy brown hair while hers was nearly the color of pitch. Her skin held more olive than theirs too, and Kelly still had to put sunscreen on if he spent longer than a half-hour outside.

"Daddy sat me and Kelly down and told us that Darla was suing him. He said she wanted more alimony, and that the success of the stud farm supported it."

Lisa's mouth dropped open, and her mother's sudden

appearance when Daddy had died suddenly made so much more sense.

"It doesn't surprise me that Daddy didn't tell you," Bruce said. "He never wanted you to think anything bad about Darla." He offered her a weak smile, but Lisa was still processing.

"Anyway," he said with a sigh. "He was worried she might actually get something from him, which would only take from the three of us. We were dealing with the Wheeler lawsuit too, and it felt like everyone wanted a piece of us— especially all these pretty women. I guess Kelly and I...we just transferred that vitriol onto you, because the moment Daddy got sick, you started asking questions about the farm, his bank accounts, his will, the estate..."

Lisa's defenses felt as high as a skyscraper. "Someone has to take care of all of that," she said through nearly clenched teeth. "I didn't mean anything—"

"I know that," Bruce said. "But it was easy to put all of my frustration on you, and then when we found out Daddy had never updated his will, we questioned whether or not he even should."

Lisa didn't know what else to say. She ran this farm, and everyone knew it. Bruce and Kelly knew it. *Of course* she should be included in the will.

"Daddy just hadn't gotten to it," she said. "Sometimes I think he thought he was bulletproof; he thought he'd live forever."

"He did act like that sometimes," Bruce admitted, a smile dancing across his face for a moment. "Anyway, I can't speak for Kelly, but I came today to talk, and part of that was to apologize for the past year." He nodded like a few words could make up for the snubs, the sneers, and the abandonment. "I really am sorry, Lisa. You love this farm the best and the most out of all of us, and I'm glad Daddy made sure you had the majority ownership of it."

He exhaled and put both hands on his knees as if he needed them to push himself into a standing position. "I contract with the Williams brothers to keep all the buildings maintained. They come out once a month and inspect everything. I try to come with them, and we usually stay out of everyone's way. I'd meet with Daddy afterward and let him know what construction or repairs, if any, was going to happen, and he'd put it in his calendar. So I guess, if that works for you, we can keep doing it that way."

Lisa started to speak, but the words stuck in her dry throat. She swallowed and managed to say, "That works for me, Bruce."

He looked at Duke, their eyes holding for several long moments. "You think you can handle her?"

"I'm sure I can't," Duke said with a grin. "But I sure am gonna try."

Bruce smiled too, and Duke stood up to shake his hand. "You make a cute couple," he said, glancing at Lisa as he pulled his hand away from Duke. "If you're going to do the traditional marriage and all of that, I'd walk you down the aisle if you wanted."

Lisa blinked, the world turning white for a moment. "I haven't thought about it a whole lot," she admitted.

"No pressure," Bruce said. He took a halting step toward her, then covered the remaining couple of feet in a rush. He hugged her tightly, and Lisa's hard-fought composure fell off a cliff. She cried into her half-brother's chest, because he was the man who'd always been in her corner previously. He'd been on her side. She'd missed him so much.

The bricks she'd built between her and the world crumbled a little bit right there in the living room, and when Bruce released her, Lisa felt like she'd just ripped off a bandage and the air was assaulting an open wound.

"I better get goin'," Bruce said. "Belinda sent me to the store for orange juice." With another smile and another nod, he left the house. With the clicking of the front door as it closed, Lisa turned back to Duke.

"If it's that easy to tell people we're getting married," she said. "Let's start spreading the word."

Duke nodded past her toward the front of the house. "I think you just did, Miss Harvey."

Her first instinct was to lash out and swat his chest. As she did, she said, "Don't call me Miss Harvey. It makes me feel eighty years old and like I'm living in the eighteen hundreds."

Duke chuckled and dodged her next swat. She lunged toward him, but he caught her hand around the wrist and pulled her into his chest. The moment sobered, though his eyes still shone with laughter. "Do you really want to marry me?" he asked. "You think you can fall in love with me eventually?"

Lisa studied his face, marveling at how quickly he could take something from fun and flirty to serious and sober.

"Yes," she whispered, and that single, three-letter word had never been harder to say. In her mind, more bricks and stones and all the mortar keeping them together came crashing down as the walls she'd built to keep everyone out started to fall apart.

"Yes, I think I can fall in love with you eventually."

CHAPTER 11

Conrad Chappell picked up his leather jacket from where he'd draped it over the back of the kitchen chair. He hung onto the end of his sleeves as he slipped his arms into the jacket. Abby Rushton had said she loved him in black leather, and while he'd gone out with her a couple of times, there wasn't really a spark between them.

On their third date in as many nights, Conrad found himself annoyed by her laugh more than anything else. The way she giggled over simply everything drove him insane, and when he'd dropped her off that night, he'd said he didn't think things were going to work out between them.

She'd dang near slammed her screen door in his face, and Conrad really thought he'd be better at ending things with women by now.

He'd told Ian about the encounter, which had been a

huge mistake. Ian had gone into a thirty-minute tirade about the unpredictability of women, and how they couldn't be trusted. How men had to set their feelings aside or risk the female wrath, and on and on.

Conrad understood where Ian currently was, and where he needed to get to in order to understand why Conrad would want to have a girlfriend. Then a wife. For a while there after Ian's divorce, Conrad felt like everything that was happening to his brother was happening to him too.

He and Ian were so tight, and they spent so much time together. They'd always gotten along really well, which made the work around Bluegrass enjoyable and the hours short. The problem, though, was that Ian had shared a lot with Conrad about what his first wife had done.

Everyone in the family knew she'd only married him for his money, but Conrad knew more.

"Who are you going out with tonight?"

Conrad turned from his thoughts and the kitchen and faced his brother. Ian removed his work gloves and tossed them in the basket where the two brothers kept things. Now that it was just the two of them in the corner house, it didn't need to be cleaned nearly as often. Duke was a real tornado around the house, leaving debris everywhere he happened to touch down.

Conrad did miss living with Lawrence, and he'd brought a calm energy to the four-some that they sorely needed.

"It's a blind date," he said. "I guess her name is June."

"You're meeting her somewhere?" Ian stepped over to

the sink and started washing his hands. He pushed his shirt-sleeves up to his elbow and then scrubbed all the way up there too. They'd been working out in the mud today, and that stuff had a special ability to get *everywhere*.

"She's a friend of Mariah's," Conrad said, wishing he'd left the house before Ian had returned. "I'm doubling with her and Lawrence."

"Mm." Ian wasn't happy about that, as he made that humming sound every time he was biting back on crueler words.

"I'm late," Conrad said, because he didn't want to start the evening off with negative vibes. Getting set up was hard enough, and he normally hated blind dates with the force of gravity. Desperate times had definitely called for desperate measures, and he'd stumbled into Lawrence and Mariah as they'd been horseback riding yesterday.

One thing had led to another, and he headed out to his truck to go to the homestead, where he'd meet up with Lawrence. They were planning to drive into town together, where yes, they'd meet Mariah and June at Stewed and Souped.

He didn't consider soup a meal in any sense of the word, but he was willing to make the concession if it meant he wouldn't have to dance with himself at Lawrence's wedding, an event that was coming up in just fourteen weeks.

His nerve endings felt like someone had thrown them in the garbage disposal and flipped it on, but he forced himself to drive down the dirt road and around the bend. The big, blue barn came into view, and he automatically looked left. Across the road that way sat Trey and Beth's house, and he thought about how Trey had come to date her simply by being the one who took TJ home all the time.

Conrad needed an easy, transitional relationship like that. He racked his brain for any female friends he had, but the only ones that came to mind were the cowgirls and female trainers that worked at Bluegrass. He'd never been attracted to any of them, and pure frustration rose up within him.

As he made another turn to go along the front of the ranch toward the road that then would take him up to the homestead, he thought about the women he knew from church. Again, no one stood out to him, and if he ever went anywhere but the ranch or the chapel, he might have better luck finding the right woman for him.

He'd gone to talk to Duke last week, only to find him locked in an intimate embrace with Lisa Harvey. After apologizing profusely, and Duke grumbling about needing a lock on his office door, Conrad had confessed he needed some help in how to meet women. Lisa, who'd perched on Duke's lap in the tiny office because Conrad had taken the chair at Lawrence's desk, had suggested Conrad try an online dating app.

He hadn't been able to bring himself to do that yet, though. To him, it almost felt like cheating, and he wasn't sure why. It was just another way to meet people.

Lawrence sat in his truck, the exhaust white and floating

up into the wintry, night air. Conrad hurried to park and switch vehicles, climbing into the passenger seat with a "Sorry, I'm late."

"You're not," he said. "Ginny and Cayden just got back this afternoon, and I wanted to stay out of the way." Lawrence flashed Conrad a smile and put his phone in the console. "You ready for this?"

"I guess," Conrad said, realizing he had let some measure of negativity infect him.

"You're going to like June," Lawrence said. "She's nice, she's employed, she's professional." He flipped the truck into reverse and started to back out of the driveway.

Conrad let Lawrence move through his music, and he didn't panic until they pulled into Mariah's driveway and both women stood from the top step of the porch.

"Wait, wait," he said. "I thought we were meeting them there."

"We were, but Mariah and June worked late, so they just came here real quick." Lawrence looked at Conrad like he'd grown horns. "You've been out with dozens of women. Probably a hundred or more. You're worried about this one?"

"You make me sound like a player," Conrad said crossly. "And yes, if you must know, I'm trying to do things a little differently now. I'm not just dating for fun." It certainly wasn't as fun, that was for dang sure.

"Well, then, come meet June and stop growling at me." Lawrence got out of the truck and received Mariah as she flew laughing into his arms. Conrad got out more slowly and rounded the front of the truck.

"Evenin', Mariah," he said, reaching up to tip his hat to Lawrence's fiancée. His gaze switched to the strawberry blonde woman coming up beside her. She was cute, but Conrad wasn't looking for *cute*, if his experience with Abby had been any indication. "You must be June."

"She is," Mariah said quickly. "June, this is Conrad Chappell, Lawrence's brother."

"Nice to meet you," June said, a very professional clip to her tone.

"All right, let's go," Lawrence said. "If you're not on time for your slot, they move the next group into it."

"At a soup place?" June asked.

"It's family-style," Mariah said, and if Conrad had known that, he'd have refused to go. His mood worsened by the minute, especially as Mariah dominated the conversation and kept drawing June's attention to the front seat of the cab and leaving him in the back alone.

He smiled through it all though, even when he had to cram himself into the corner at the restaurant. June sat beside him, but she was practically on top of him, the awkwardness between them astronomical.

Lawrence used to go on plenty of blind dates, and Conrad didn't know how he'd done it. This was pure torture.

About halfway through the meal, after he'd seen a child of about ten dip his spoon into the community pot, lick it, and then go back for more, Conrad couldn't stand sitting at the table for another moment.

"I'll be right back," he said, though June had barely spoken to him. The conversation had been a group affair, with the two women really talking to each other while Conrad and Lawrence were forced to eat things like bisque and gazpacho.

He managed to get past everyone else at the table that practically touched the wall behind it and head for the bathrooms. He wondered if he could sneak out the window in there, the way he'd seen plenty of people do in movies and on TV shows.

Unfortunately, the men's restroom had no window, and Conrad was left to contemplate the reality of climbing up into the vent in the ceiling. If he stood on the toilet, he could probably reach it...

"This is how you know your night isn't going well," he grumbled to himself. He washed his hands, seriously considering texting Lawrence that he'd grab a cab to get back to the ranch, and left the men's room with his mind occupied somewhere else.

Therefore, he didn't see the waitress as she rushed toward the swinging, plastic door that led into the kitchen.

"James!" she screeched before she'd even reached the door. That voice brought Conrad's head up at the same moment the waitress realized they were about to collide.

He managed to lift one hand before she plowed right into him, a very full, very hot bowl of soup in her hand. Hot liquid seeped right through his light blue dress shirt, and the color of the curry didn't really go with his look for that evening.

A bright yellow stain spread across his abdomen and dripped down the front of his pants. He stared at the soup as it dripped onto the floor and the clattering of the bowl finally came to a stop.

CHAPTER 12

Ryanne Moon stared at the mess she'd just made. It seemed to match her life, right down to the putrid yellow color of the ginger curry soup she'd just smashed into a cowboy's chest.

"Oh, my goodness," she said, clapping one hand over her mouth as the reality of the situation caught up to her. "I'm so sorry. I didn't see you, and that customer had just screamed at me for bringing the soup he ordered, and—"

She cut off when she looked into the dark eyes of Conrad Chappell.

Send an earthquake, she thought. *A tornado. Open the ground and let it swallow me whole. I don't care.*

She continued to petition the Lord to send the worst natural disaster he could, just to the four-foot-square where she stood. *Spare everyone else, but please, please get me out of here.*

"Ryanne?" he asked.

A laugh started somewhere in the bottom of her stomach, rising through her core and gaining hysteria with every inch. A manic laugh came shooting out of her mouth, and Ry clapped her hand over the sound, trying to mute it.

He didn't smile or look particularly happy to see her. Why should he? She'd literally just stained his very expensive clothing. She instantly looked back at the blue shirt. Ruined. "You can send me the bill," she said. She could replace that shirt with one from her men's collection—a fitted one—and Conrad Chappell would look like a million bucks.

He already did, though, as he'd always possessed a devil-may-care type of handsomeness that very few men could pull off.

"I will," he said, looking down at himself again. "Although, you might have just saved me from a very uncomfortable situation."

"Is that right?" she asked, crouching to pick up the now-empty bowl. Kayley would have to come mop up this mess, and someone opened the kitchen door, nearly slipped in the spilled soup, and called for the sanitation department to come get this area cleaned up.

"This isn't a great place, Ry," Janice said, as if Ryanne didn't know.

She wanted to throw the bowl at her supervisor's head. Instead, she smiled and said, "If you could tell everyone to go out the other door, that would be great." She fluttered her eyelashes a few times, and Janice just nodded. She went back inside, already yelling with that monster-loud voice of hers for everyone to use the other exit from the kitchen until this one could be cleaned up.

"What uncomfortable situation?" Ry asked Conrad.

He blinked. "What?"

"You said this might have saved you from an uncomfortable situation." She knew what it was before he spoke. The only reason men came to Stewed and Souped was to impress their women. Or they'd lost a bet. She pinned a smile to her face, though she wanted to scream. "Let me guess. Your date's not going well?"

She nodded toward the bathrooms. "So you escaped, hoping the men's room would have a window." She leaned closer, feeling dangerous and unstable. Maybe slightly crazed. "The owner specifically told the builders no windows in the men's room. The women's room, however...one whole wall of windows."

He looked at her with all the soberness in the world before he burst out laughing. Ry joined him, remembering so many things about this man. They might be nineteen or twenty years old, but the memories were good.

Kayley appeared with her mop and bucket, frowning at the horrible soup on the floor.

"Sorry," Ry said. "This guy came at me out of nowhere."

"Totally my fault," Conrad said, stepping back out of the way. "Do you happen to have any wipes or anything? Maybe one of those chemical wash stations I can just step into?" He gave Ry a playful look, his eyes dancing with what she could only call delight.

This might be the one bright spot of her night, and

suddenly it didn't matter that two of her tables—two!—had stiffed her on the tip and that she had twenty-nine clothing orders to pull, wrap, and package so they'd be ready to mail in the morning.

She couldn't sleep until those packages were ready, because her online clothing company promised next-day mailings for subscribers. It was one of the many benefits of paying twenty-five dollars a month and being able to select one garment from a pool of four carefully cultivated, readily available, modern styles.

Ry was literally one day away from putting in her two weeks' notice here at Stewed and Souped, and she was going to take the plunge and open her online clothing store in a real brick-and-mortar building. The list of things that needed to happen before she could do that didn't allow her to keep waitressing, and for the past six months, Andy and Ryan more than paid for her bills.

The online store had grown so much since her interview last summer, but she hadn't dared to quit her job. She was ready now. Beyond ready, if nights like this were going to keep happening.

She wouldn't mind the reintroduction of a sexy cowboy to her life, though. At the same time, Ry's mind shouted at her that she didn't have time for a boyfriend. She barely had time to sleep.

Before she knew it, Conrad was walking away from her and into the kitchen, where they did have an industrial sink with a long hose he could use to clean up. She wondered what he'd do—take off his shirt and hose himself down?

Her whole body grew hot, because she'd run into him, and he'd been one solid piece of man. She looked around, realizing that Kayley was now mopping up the last of the soup and she stood there alone, holding a dirty soup bowl and staring at the black plastic door.

The heat in her body turned embarrassed, and she quickly palmed her way into the kitchen. She tossed the dirty bowl on the platform next to the dishwasher and continued toward the back of the room, where the big prep sinks were.

Conrad stood at one of them, leaning forward while he used the hose to spray his shirt. "I'm not sure this is working," he yelled over the noise in the kitchen.

"You should take it off," she called back. "Or just go home."

She turned away from him and grabbed a clean towel from a shelf. He hadn't taken his shirt off, much to her dismay, when she turned back to him, but he held the hose for her to wet the towel. She wrung it out and started dabbing at the outer edge of the stain on his shirt.

"I'll let you do the pants," she said, backing away from the man she'd once known as a teenager. He'd been big and broad then, and she'd been attracted to him physically just like she was now. They'd gone out a few times, and he'd taken her to their junior prom. He'd kissed her that night, and Ry found herself thrown back almost twenty years, to a night much more magical than this one.

All of a sudden, her fantasy memories came to a screeching halt. She had gone out with Conrad Chappell.

They'd started to become a couple. Then summer had come, and he'd said he didn't have time to date over the summer. His father was a brutal taskmaster, and Conrad had some class or training or something he had to attend in Louisville.

They'd drifted apart and broken up. The next thing Ryanne knew, though, was that Conrad had a new girl-friend, and she lived only two blocks from Ryanne. He drove by her house every dang day after that, and Ry had never felt so stupid or so unworthy.

That definitely cooled her jets, and she fell back even further. "Sorry about the shirt," she said. "And the pants. Make sure you send me a bill."

She started to walk away, but he said, "Ryanne?" in that smooth, sexy, cowboy voice of his.

She pressed her eyes closed and walled off her hormones. She'd only reacted to him the way she had because she hadn't been out with anyone in a while. A boyfriend? She'd have to look up the definition of the word to remember what one was.

"Yes?" she bit through her teeth.

"How will I get in touch with you?" he asked, his eyes doing that dancing thing again. "You better give me your number so I can send you the bill."

"Fine," she said, and she rattled off the number.

He typed it into his phone, smiled, and said, "I might not bother trying to clean them, but I'll find comparable prices for you."

"You do that," she said, and she finally got away from him. She couldn't wait for this night to end, but even when it did, he still stuck in her mind. He stayed while she packaged all of her orders, and he stayed while she brushed her teeth.

She finally lay down in bed, completely spent and wishing it wasn't three a.m. when Conrad Chappell appeared in her mind. Ryanne smiled into the darkness before she realized she had nothing to smile about when it came to him.

Nothing at all.

Chapter 13

Duke moved his hand from Lisa's waist and slid it up her side, eventually cradling her face. He really enjoyed it when she dropped by his office unannounced, especially when she let him kiss her before she left.

"I really have to go," she murmured, but she didn't even attempt to open the door.

He put his hand flat against the door and kissed her again, feeling slightly out of control. The past three weeks with her had been fairly intense, as he'd gone over to her farm almost every day to help her clean things out.

Wayne Harvey sure had been a packrat—and not that clean. Sometimes, Duke could still feel the dust on his fingers and he'd have to wash his hands to convince himself he wasn't covered in dirt and cobwebs.

She'd gotten the skunks removed from under the deck,

and her relationship with Bruce and Kelly and their wives had started to improve.

Duke had learned that everything having to do with relationships and Lisa Harvey moved slow, as she was like molasses in January when it came to admitting things, forgiving others, and letting people in.

He'd been chipping away at her for what felt like a long time for him, and he had to remind himself that not everyone fell in love as quickly as he did. Not everyone got their heart crushed *because* they fell in love as quickly as he did.

"Don't you have class in five minutes?" she asked, putting one hand against his chest and pressing him back a couple of inches.

"Yes," he said, clearing his throat. He opened his eyes and looked at Lisa, the dazzling smile on her face telling him she liked kissing him too. "You're still on-board for going to dinner with my parents tomorrow?"

They'd planned a meal at the house around the bend to tell his parents they were getting married...in only ten days.

No one else knew, at least not in the Chappell family. Lisa had told her half-brothers, because they already knew about the marriage stipulation, and they all figured they better get the will and estate wrapped up as soon as possible.

Her smile slipped. "Yes," she said. "Six o'clock?"

"I can come get you," he said, falling back into the office. He retreated to his desk and picked up the notebook where he kept track of everything to do with the breeding at Bluegrass. His busy season was nearly upon him, and Duke's anxiety sprung through him. How was he going to manage getting married, moving, and then commuting to Bluegrass to oversee all the covering? Not to mention the two courses he'd signed up for this term...

He swallowed back the intense feelings of exhaustion and of being completely overwhelmed. When he felt like this, all he wanted to do was pick up a video game controller and lose himself for hours. That wouldn't help anything, because then he'd be even further behind in the work he needed to do.

"Or you can meet me at the homestead," he said. "You don't have to show up alone." He looked up and found her studying him.

"You're frowning," she said, taking a step toward him. "Why?"

Duke let a sigh hiss from between his lips. "I'm just a little overwhelmed right now." He erased the tension riding his eyebrows and smiled at her. "Really, I'm fine."

"Look who's boxing things up now," she teased, those dark eyes sending sparks at him.

He chuckled and ducked his head. "I probably am. I just have two classes this term. And getting married, and moving into your place, and..." He shook his head. "It's okay. Covering season is always like this. I just take it one task at a time."

"What can I do to help you?" Lisa spoke in a tender, kind voice, and she brushed her fingertips along Duke's jaw.

He met her eyes, something powerful firing through him. He'd taken her to dinner several times. They'd walked around the mall for one of their dates. He liked talking to her and learning more about her, but they had leagues to go before he could truly say he loved her.

It still felt like love pumping through his veins with every beat of his heart.

"Let me come pick you up tomorrow night." He swept one hand along her waist and pulled her flush against him. "If I come at five, you can tell me if the tuxedo looks okay."

She grinned at him and put both hands against his chest. "I'm sure it looks *fabulous*."

"Did you find a dress?" he whispered, tracing his nose down her cheek.

"I'm picking it up tomorrow," she said.

"Can I see it?"

"No," she said with a light laugh. "That's bad luck, Duke."

"I didn't realize we were playing by all the rules of a traditional wedding."

"Well, we are." She pushed against him again, and he released her.

"I told you I'd like it if you wore those jeans and whatever shirt you wanted." He glanced down the length of her body. Mm hm, those jeans and those boots would do just fine for getting married. She wore a red jacket today, so he couldn't see what her shirt looked like, and he envisioned maybe a white blouse with flowers on it would be nice for saying I-do.

"Now you've made me late for a phone call I need to make," she said with mock anger. "And you're late for class."

"Who are you calling?" he asked, stepping past her to open the door for her.

"Johnny Loveless," she said. "He's finally setting up appointments for Luck Be A Lady."

"Wow," Duke said, recognizing the name of the Belmont winner from last year. "Good for him."

"I swear, he's been holding out on purpose." Lisa shook her head as they went outside.

"Sounds like someone else I know," he quipped, and she spun back to him.

"You take that back," she said, something dangerous sparking in those dark eyes. "I came back and apologized to you, Duke Chappell." She actually shook one fist in his direction, and Duke danced out of the way.

He burst out laughing, grabbed onto her wrist, and spun her around as if he'd taken her dancing. She squealed, and when he brought her back to him, she grabbed onto him and started to laugh too.

Not giggle, thankfully. Lisa Harvey didn't giggle, and Duke liked that. His phone rang, and he pulled it from his pocket with one hand while keeping his hold on Lisa with the other. "It's Lance," he said. "He's in my finance class. He's probably wondering where I am."

"Go," she said. "I'll see you tomorrow." She started to walk away.

"Five?" Duke asked, and Lisa waved her hand above her head to say yes. Duke swiped on the call and said, "Hey, Lance. I'm just running a little behind with getting off the ranch." He turned away from Lisa's retreating feminine form and headed in the opposite direction to get back to the homestead.

"All right," Duke said, flying down the stairs in his shiny, black cowboy boots. He only wore these to weddings, and he couldn't believe the next one would be his. As the youngest Chappell, he'd fully expected to do everything last. "What do you think?"

Lisa looked up from her phone and rose to her feet from where she'd been sitting at the kitchen table. In some miracle, no one else had been in the homestead when they'd returned. Duke knew Lawrence was off with Mariah tonight, and they were picking out the meal they'd serve at their spring wedding.

He had no idea where Cayden and Ginny were, as they both worked busy jobs, and apparently Ginny had *two* other homes.

Anyone could walk in at any time, but all Duke had to do was turn and race back up the steps if they did.

Lisa's eyes took in every inch of him, and Duke felt it keenly as his skin started to itch and prickle.

"It's too big, isn't it?" he asked. "I've lost a little weight this month." He had too, and he wasn't sure why. He ate the same, and he worked the same. He didn't work out specifically, because the work around the ranch was enough to keep him trim and decently fit.

He smoothed down the jacket, which did billow a little

bit as it tapered from his shoulders to his waist. He couldn't get a smaller size, though, or else it wouldn't fit across his shoulders.

"It's just not right," Lisa said.

"I know." Duke drew in a breath and sighed, looking up to meet her eyes. "Are you sure we can't just wear normal clothes?"

"You just want to get married in jeans."

"Yes," he said. "I do." He tried smiling at her, and she actually gave him a small smile back.

She approached and brushed her hand across his right shoulder and down that arm. "I'll admit it doesn't suit you."

"I'll buy brand-new jeans," he said. "I'll wear a black shirt with long sleeves and a tie in any color you want. I think you said you wanted pale pink, navy blue, and silver, right? I can find a tie like that. I've got a real nice black dress hat. I'll look good, I swear."

Lisa had started nodding as he'd mentioned the colors. She didn't stop when he quit speaking. She circled him, her fingers trailing along his back and sending desire straight through him. She honestly had no idea what she did to him, and Duke stood very still to make sure she didn't.

"All right," she finally said. "I can live with you in jeans, those boots, a black shirt, and a really nice tie. The hat. Polish up your belt buckle." She came to stand in front of him again. "You are a very good-looking cowboy, Duke."

A smile exploded onto his face. "Lisa Harvey," he teased. "Did you just compliment me?"

She shook her head as she smiled. "I compliment you."

"I can tell you're thinking it," he said. "And you let me hold your hand and kiss you, but you're not real wordy with the compliments."

Her smile slipped. "I can do better at that."

"It's okay," he said. "I know you do things to show how you feel. I say things."

"You say enough for both of us," she said dryly.

Duke laughed and turned toward the steps. "You wanna see the shirt and hat, at least?"

"Yeah, we've got time."

Duke dashed back upstairs, and he'd never been happier to ditch his tux. He pulled on a pair of clean jeans, the black shirt, which he paired with a blue, white, and purple tie, and put his boots back on.

He got down the hat box from the top of his closet, and he removed the hat he only wore for special occasions. With that in place, he headed back downstairs, his boots making enough noise to wake the dead.

"Okay," he said, realizing a beat too late that Lisa stood talking to someone else. His eyes moved past her to Olli.

Duke's heart sunk all the way to his fancy cowboy boots. Where Olli was, Spur was sure to follow, and sure enough, two male voices came down the hall that led back to the master bedroom.

Spur and Cayden.

Great, Duke thought, now frozen to the spot.

They entered the living area of the house in the next moment, and he wouldn't have been able to escape even if he'd spun and run.

"Let me have the baby," Ginny said, following the cowboys, and she hurried over to Olli's side.

"Why are you all dressed up nice?" Spur asked, coming toward Duke. He grabbed him in a hug and Duke clapped him on the back.

"Oh, uh..." Duke looked at Lisa, who only smiled at him. She'd erased all emotion from her face, and that meant Duke was on his own.

They were going to find out anyway. He didn't want to lie to anyone. He extended his hand toward Lisa, and she seemed to get the whole conversation in an instant. He liked that, and as she slipped her fingers through his, he drew in a strengthening breath.

"We're going to dinner with Mom and Daddy tonight," he said. "So you have to keep this to yourselves for a few hours. Can you do that?"

"Spur's terrible with secrets," Olli said. "We're just going to dinner with Cayden and Ginny, so we can probably waste a couple of hours without saying anything."

"I'll take his phone," Cayden said, moving to stand next to Spur, which was only an arm's length from Duke and Lisa.

They exchanged a glance, and Duke said, "Okay. Lisa and I are getting married. On February second."

The homestead sat in silence for a couple of seconds. Duke watched the shock roll across his brothers' faces, and he watched as Olli and Ginny tried to count the days until February second.

"That's only nine days away," Ginny finally said, her hand coming up to cover her mouth.

"That's right," Duke said. "Nine days. So keep your mouth shut for a few more hours, and I'm sure Mom will text out the details."

CHAPTER 14

Lisa's foot would not stop bouncing. The drive from the homestead to Duke's parents' house only took five minutes down a dirt road that wrapped around the front of the ranch. But she felt like it was a death march she was making one slow breath at a time.

"It's going to be okay," he said as he pulled into the long driveway.

The house stood tall in the night, with lights illuminating every eave. It looked like a custom home, which of course it was. Everything the Chappells did was custommade for them, right down to the tiny office Duke shared with Lawrence in what should've been a horse stable.

The garage was separate from the rest of the house, with a catwalk of roof over the short sidewalk connecting them. The house rose for two stories, and it had a tall, pointed roof and a bright red front door.

"I haven't met anyone's parents before," she admitted.

"Neither have I," he said.

"Really? You've never had a serious girlfriend?" She turned toward him. "You told me you dated a lot."

"Dating a lot implies that the relationships are shallow," Duke said without looking at her. He too studied the house, and that didn't bring her any comfort. "Mom knows we're here. Might as well go in." He sounded resigned to getting something over with, and Lisa wasn't sure if that bothered her or not.

She waited for him to come open her door, and she slipped down to the driveway and took his hand. "Do you get along with your parents?"

He walked slowly toward the sidewalk. "Daddy, yes, most of the time. He was pretty strict growing up; he expected us to be up at four a.m. with him, working for hours before school. There were chores after school too, and there was never any question that all eight of us would work the ranch."

"Interesting," Lisa said. "And not one of you broke ranks?"

"Not one of us," he said. "Yet." He shrugged slightly. "I guess Trey kind of has. He doesn't live here anymore, and he works at Bluegrass part-time at best. He's been focused on his wife's farm and property since they got married."

Lisa wondered if that would happen with Duke too. He worked a ton here at Bluegrass, and she wasn't sure how he'd be able to do anything at Horses by Harvey. She wasn't even sure she wanted him to.

Just something else you need to talk about, she told herself.

That list grew with every day that passed, and Lisa wasn't all that great at starting deep or meaningful conversations. Just tonight, though, she'd added two things: his desire for a family and where he saw himself working in the future.

She thought of the beautiful baby boy Olivia Chappell had held in her arms. Lisa had never considered herself all that maternal, but she sure did like the sweet, powdery scent of a baby, and she'd liked stroking the baby's soft, downy, black hair that Olli claimed had just started growing.

Duke led her up the steps and knocked on the door as he opened it. "Hello," he called. "We're here."

His mother looked up from the back of the house, which was deeper than it was wide. The kitchen took up the whole back of the house, with a table on the right where someone would come in from the garage.

Duke took her past a sectional couch in the living room to the long island in the kitchen. His mom rounded that, her smile as bright as noonday on a clear day in July. "Hello, Duke," she said, and she almost sounded fake and so South-ern-proper. She embraced him, and he let go of Lisa's hand to hug his mother.

Lisa smiled at the pair of them, because joy did radiate off his mom. She released him and turned to Lisa. "Hello, Lisa."

"Mom," Duke said as his mom started to swoop toward her. "You didn't even let me introduce her."

"Go on, go on." His mother paused and backed up, her lighter eyes dazzling and dancing.

"Lisa, this is my mother, Julie," he said. "Mom, this is my

—" He cleared his throat, obviously not thinking through the introduction all that much. "Fiancée," he said. "She's my fiancée, Lisa Harvey."

"Fiancée?" Julie screeched, her eyes rounding and all the happiness draining out of them as she turned toward her son.

"Who's a fiancée?" a man asked, and everyone turned toward the older gentleman entering the kitchen.

"Daddy," Duke said, stepping back to make room in the little circle they'd made. "This is Lisa Harvey, Wayne's daughter. We're engaged."

His father stopped at the end of the island and put one hand on it as if he needed it to steady himself. "Engaged?" He looked past Duke to Lisa. "You two are engaged?"

"Yes," Duke said, stepping to Lisa's side and backing away from the island. "There's more. We're, um, getting married in just over a week."

"My goodness," Julie said, pressing one hand to her heart as if saluting the flag. Shock filled every syllable. "What happened?" Her eyes dropped to Lisa's midsection, and embarrassed heat filled her face.

Lisa had asked Duke not to tell anyone about the stipulation in the will, but her decision on that wavered. Her half-brothers knew. Maybe Duke's parents should too.

"Can you keep a secret?" Lisa asked. She hadn't even shaken any hands yet or received any hugs. She wasn't much of a hugger—unless it was Duke taking her into his arms—but she thought she'd probably like a hug from his mother.

Darla had been in town for a few days, but her hugs felt

like embracing cardboard. There was no love there, and Julie felt full of the stuff.

She hadn't said, "Nice to meet you," or "My father spoke so highly of you, sir," the way she'd planned.

She looked back and forth between Julie and her husband, whose name Lisa knew was Jefferson. Daddy had liked Jefferson Chappell a lot, and he'd told Lisa way back when he'd first started training her to be their scheduler that the Chappells sat at the top of the list. They had great horses, and great history, and great heritage.

Always take an appointment with Bluegrass, Daddy had said.

"I can," Jefferson said. "That one's a bit of a mystery. She might keep it, and she might not." He smiled at his wife, who simply frowned at him.

"We're getting married," Duke said, meeting Lisa's eye. "Because we'd started dating a little bit before Lisa's daddy died."

"Sort of," Lisa said. "He just brought pie and flirted with me."

"Hey, I think *you* were flirting with me." Duke grinned at her, and some of the tension in the house released. "Anyway." He squeezed her hand, and she'd never been more grateful to have someone at her side.

Maybe she really didn't have to do everything alone.

"You fell in love with her in two seconds flat." Julie folded her arms, the look on her face only made of disgust now.

"I did not," Duke said defensively, and Lisa saw instantly what the issue was between him and his mother.

"My daddy's will said I have to be married in order to inherit the stud farm. Since Duke and I...we've talked a lot about it, and we both think this relationship can be something amazing. We're just..." She looked at him, because he'd explained it so well.

"Speeding things up a little," he said, immediately clearing his throat. "I did not fall in love with her in two seconds, Mother." He glared in his mom's direction. "But I do think I *can* fall in love with her, and we've decided that she needs to get the farm sooner rather than later, and so we're getting married on February second."

After a beat of silence, Jefferson started chuckling. The sound started out low and slow, but it grew and grew into something loud and rambunctious. Lisa smiled at him, because at least laughing wasn't yelling.

She looked at Julie. Or the silent, brooding disapproval pouring from her. A timer went off on her stove, and she still didn't move. She kept her arms folded across her burgundy blouse, which she'd paired with a long, floor-length skirt that seemed like the perfect thing to wear to meet her son's fiancée.

"Come on, Momma," Jefferson said, limping into the kitchen to silence the timer. "The boy is going to do what he wants to do. It worked out for Trey and Beth." He pressed the button, and the beeping stopped.

"Trey and Beth?" Lisa asked.

"Right," Duke said. "They got married so she could

enter her horse into the Sweetheart Classic. It wasn't really real at first."

"It wasn't real *at all* at first," Julie bit out.

"And they made it work into something real," Duke threw back at her. "I don't need your permission, Mom. We're here, because I wanted you to know, and I want you both at the wedding, and I'm almost thirty-three years old. I haven't rushed into anything, and we've spent the last three and a half weeks talking everything to death."

His mother's face softened, and Lisa's heart went out to her, and then Duke. They clearly had some history there, and he really didn't like her assumptions about him.

"This is done, baby," Jefferson said. "I can't get it out and balance."

That got his mother to move, and he came back around the island the other way while she pulled something that smelled browned, meaty, and delicious out of the oven.

Jefferson came right over to Duke and Lisa, engulfing both of them in a huge hug, one arm around Duke and one around Lisa. "I could've gotten that roast out," he whispered. "You owe me for getting her over there." A low rumble chuckled through his chest, and Lisa could only smile at the gentle giant this man was.

He didn't seem like the strict taskmaster Duke had described ten minutes ago.

"Thanks, Daddy," Duke said, stepping back. "You can be there on the second?"

"Where is this wedding?" Jefferson asked in a louder voice.

"Right here on the ranch," Duke said. "I scheduled the pavilion. We don't need anything fancy." He looked at Lisa, such hope in his eyes. "I'm still tryin' to get Lisa to let us ride horses in."

She grinned at him, because the man had a way of getting exactly what he wanted, and if he dug at her enough, she'd probably relent to the horses.

"You're getting married outside in the winter?" Julie asked, plenty of incredulity in her voice. "Duke, we're old. We can't sit outside in the winter while you ride on in on a horse." She clucked her tongue and kept her focus on basting the beef roast she'd removed from the oven. "Olli and Spur have tiny Gus, and there's no way they can keep him outside."

"It'll be fast," Duke said, releasing Lisa's hand. "Ten minutes. How long does it take to get married?"

"We all have to gather. There's the wedding party." His mom drew out the last word over the R-sound. "The music. Will you feed everyone? Dance after? What is this wedding going to look like?"

"Mom," Duke said. "Will you calm down? Breathe for a second."

"I'm sure Duke knows what he's doing," his daddy said, both eyebrows raised toward the stars. "Or he wouldn't have shown up here nine days before the wedding to tell us he's getting married."

"We know what we're doing," Duke said, gesturing to the table. "Can we tell you while we eat? I'm starving."

"That boy is always starving," Julie said as she set the

now-carved roast on the table. She returned to the kitchen to get a bowl of mashed potatoes, and then a casserole dish with roasted vegetables in it. "I hope you know that, Lisa."

"I've seen him eat," she said with a smile. Duke pulled out her chair for her, but Lisa didn't take it quite yet. As Julie came back to the table, Lisa stepped in front of her. "It sure is nice to meet you, ma'am. Duke's talked a lot about his parents."

Hesitatingly, and a little jerkily, she stepped forward and hugged Julie Chappell.

"Well, I'll be," Jefferson drawled.

Lisa stepped out of Julie's arms and turned toward him. He'd already taken a seat, and Lisa knew he'd had hip surgery a while ago that had left him with a limp. "My father always spoke so highly of you, sir. He taught me to always take an appointment with Bluegrass, because y'all have great horses and are so easy to work with."

Duke scoffed under his breath, but Lisa ignored him.

"Thank you, darlin'," Jefferson said with a real wide smile on his face. "I like this one, Duke."

"You like anyone who can make peach pie too," Julie quipped, taking her seat. "Come on, now, kids. Sit, sit. It's time to eat." She acted like she'd been ready for hours, and they'd been delaying her on purpose.

Lisa took the seat Duke offered her, and he sat down last, directly across from his mother.

"All right," she said, scooping some potatoes onto her plate. "Let's hear about this wedding."

* * *

Lisa couldn't believe how fast the last eight days had passed. She looked at the bags of things she had stacked on the kitchen table. Everything was assembled and ready. She and Duke had been working on the centerpieces until twenty minutes ago, and they were finally ready.

Ginny Winters—now a Chappell—had graciously offered her mansion on Sweet Rose Whiskey property for the wedding. It had an enormous ballroom where the woman had hosted parties for hundreds that would accommodate everyone in the Chappell and Harvey families for the ceremony.

Indoors.

The giant kitchen and dining area had likewise seen plenty of dinner parties, and close family and friends would then move into that area of the mansion for a meal.

Duke had catered their wedding dinner from Michaels, which was a premier restaurant that hosted all the celebrities when they came into town for horse races, auctions, and more. Lisa had never eaten there before, and she couldn't believe the first time would be on her wedding day.

She couldn't believe *tomorrow* was her wedding day.

"Believe it," she muttered to herself as she went down the hall to her bedroom. She was not staying in the master, as she hadn't been able to throw away everything Daddy owned. She didn't want to wash the sheets and bedding, because then she'd erase the smell of him.

She'd been living in her bedroom for years, and it would

continue to work for her. It was on the main level, but there wasn't another bedroom up here. Three bedrooms, a large living area, two more bathrooms, and a partial kitchen took up the basement, and Duke would live down there.

He'd called it an apartment of its own, and it almost was. The only issue with that was that it didn't have a separate entrance, so no matter what, he'd have to come in the house on the main level to get downstairs.

Lisa's stomach rolled and pinched as she changed into her pajamas. Her dress hung in the closet, and she stared at it for a moment. It was pretty, but not a wedding gown. Duke had honestly told her a dozen times to wear jeans and her cowgirl hat, and she'd actually considered it.

Once she'd toured Ginny's mansion, though, she'd abandoned the idea. That mansion required a person to wear a gown at all times, including for a wedding.

"*Your* wedding," she said aloud to herself, staring at the dress. She turned away from it a moment later, wishing with all the energy of her heart that she had a mother or a sister to be with her that night. A best friend who could talk instead of neigh.

Someone.

As she settled into bed, she realized that come tomorrow night, she'd have someone sleeping in the house with her— her husband.

CHAPTER 15

Duke bent over to pull on his boots, noting when the door opened and men started to enter the bedroom Ginny had set up for the groom's room. After dinner with his parents last week, Duke had gone back to the homestead in a huff. That mistake had turned out to be a blessing, as Cayden and Ginny were making hot fudge in the kitchen, and Ginny was extraordinarily gifted at getting a person to talk.

He'd told them how Mom had basically disparaged all of the wedding plans, and Ginny had gently suggested they could use her mansion on Virginia Avenue. He'd called Lisa, and they'd gone to see the house the next day.

Duke knew the moment the house had come into view that Lisa would love to get married there. Her eyes had lit up with a glow he hadn't seen before, and he'd been battling guilt and regret that he couldn't give her the wedding of her dreams.

For once, he hadn't spoken the things stewing inside him, and Lisa had never said anything about what kind of wedding she wanted. When they'd talked about the wedding, she'd always said, "It's fine if it's simple. Let's not complicate anything."

He'd thought she'd been dealing with a lot—the funeral, the death of her father, running the ranch, cleaning out the house, and patching things up with her half-brothers. Adding planning a wedding to her list had probably overwhelmed her.

Duke felt the to-do list he had choking him, even now.

"There you are," Lawrence said, and Duke looked up from his shiny boots. He rose to his feet, buoyed by the brightness in his brother's smile. Lawrence took his hand and shook it, then pulled him into his chest. "I can't believe you're getting married today."

"I can't either," Duke said, his emotion barely contained in the ball in the back of his throat.

"I know you said it's not a hundred percent," Lawrence whispered. "But Duke, you should see yourself when Lisa walks in the room."

Duke didn't say anything, because Conrad and Blaine only stood four feet away. He smiled at them, squeezed Lawrence extra-tight, so appreciative that he hadn't said anything to anyone else, and stepped back. "Thanks, Lawrence."

He blew out his breath and looked around the massive bedroom. Ginny had arranged for someone to move the bed, so the room was mostly open. She'd brought in chairs and a couch so they'd have somewhere to sit once they were ready, and Duke would need to buy her all the banana ice cream she wanted for the rest of her life to repay her generosity.

Cayden had said that Ginny could make anything happen, and she definitely had. The ballroom where she hosted her parties had been likewise restructured, and the party supply store had come in with the chairs and altar that morning.

"It'll be your turn soon," he said to Lawrence.

"I'm already praying for a mild spring," Lawrence said with a pinched smile. "Mariah wants *everything* outside."

Rain had started to drizzle about an hour ago, and Duke was glad he didn't have to answer to Mom about the weather. She'd been thrilled with the change in venue, and she'd tried to step into the wedding plans every day since he'd had dinner with her.

"Congratulations," Conrad said, moving over to Duke and Lawrence. "Spur sent me in with this." He produced the boutonniere that Olli had made from the flowers she used to make her perfumes and candle scents.

Conrad grinned at him as he pinned it to Duke's lapel. "Lookin' good, brother. How'd you get her to let you wear jeans?"

"Seriously," Blaine said. "You look so comfortable." He hugged Duke too, and more people entered the room. Trey and TJ looked around, spotted Duke in the corner, and made a beeline for him.

"Uncle Duke!" TJ ran the last few steps. "Look what my

momma made for you." He thrust a quart-sized jar of dark
red sauce toward him, and Duke knew exactly what it was.

"Spaghetti sauce." He laughed and took the jar from TJ.
"You'll have to tell 'er thanks, bud." Duke bent down and
hugged TJ, then did the same with Trey.

"I talked to Mom," Trey said as they separated.

Duke met his eye, anxiety flowing through him like a
river through a canyon. "Oh?"

"She wanted me to give you some tips about this
whole..." He glanced left and right. "Marriage thing."

"Why would you give him tips and not me?" Blaine
asked. "I actually got married to a woman I loved, and who
loved me, and—oh my word." He spun to Duke. "Are you
and Lisa not really...I mean..."

Trey rolled his eyes. "Anyway," he said, as if what Blaine
had just suggested—that Duke and Lisa were getting
married for the wrong reasons—was absolutely insane. "I
told her I had no idea what she meant, and that I barely
know what I'm doing even to this day."

Duke grinned at Trey, who smiled right on back.

"We each just figure it out for ourselves," Trey said,
reaching over and clapping Blaine on the shoulder. "Right,
Blaine? Can you imagine me telling you how to deal with
Tam?"

Blaine burst out laughing and shook his head. "No way.
Tam's a special breed."

"All women are, brother," Trey said. "Which is why it
doesn't matter if it's me or you or Spur tellin' Duke how to
be married. He doesn't need that. He'll figure it out." He

nodded to Blaine, then Duke, and then he took TJ's hand, and they left the room.

"Twenty minutes," Spur said when he walked through the door. He carried Gus in his left arm, the baby cradled there like a football. "Olli, Ginny, Tam, and Beth are with Lisa, Duke. They're makin' sure she's gonna be real pretty." He grinned at Duke. "You sure you don't want to take time off? Even just a few days? Just go somewhere close. Get away."

Duke shook his head. "Lisa says she can't. She has some company meeting they do every February. We want to be here for the Sweetheart Classic. And it's covering season right after that."

"All right," Spur said, plenty of doubt in his voice. "We can cover for you for a few days at Bluegrass if you'd like. Just so you know."

"I know," Duke said, stepping into his brother and hugging him, baby Gus between them. The baby gurgled, and Duke grinned at him as he fell back. "And I appreciate it."

Daddy came into the room next, along with Mom. "This is the men's room, Mom," Spur said, going to intercept her. Apparently word had gotten around to the family that Duke hadn't appreciated the way she'd tried to change everything about his wedding, and Spur had obviously been nominated to play referee between the two of them.

"I just want that baby," Mom said, reaching for Gus. Spur passed the baby over, and Mom met Duke's eyes. She smiled at him, and he wanted to forgive her. He did love his mother. He'd feel less guilty if he just went and gave her a hug.

He did, and she gripped him with a strength he didn't know a woman as petite as her could possess. "I just want you to be happy," she whispered, her voice weak and shaky.

"I *am* happy, Mom," he said. "You were right about having a wedding outside in February. You should be happy about that."

She let out a burst of laughter that was still rimmed with tears and released him.

"It's going to be okay," he said, because he felt that way down deep in his soul. He'd felt like that since he and Lisa had decided to do this. He never did propose to her, but he did take her ring shopping, and she'd picked out a diamond she liked.

If, later on, things between them sat on stable ground, and they fell truly, madly, and deeply in love, Duke could get her the fancy diamond ring then. He could get down on both knees and pledge himself to her for the rest of his life, and ask her to be his for the rest of hers. Just because something started out one way didn't mean it had to stay that way.

Beth and Trey had had a ring ceremony last summer to really celebrate their wedding, though they'd been married for eight or nine months by then. Duke could easily do something like that if Lisa wanted to.

He didn't want to; he just wanted her to have everything she wanted. He had plenty of money to make that happen for her—if he knew what she wanted.

Sometimes, he felt like he had to pry at her to get her to give him the simplest of answers, but he'd learned a couple of her weaknesses. She loved it when he brought her coffee from her favorite shop in town, and she liked showing up in his office spontaneously and trying to catch him sleeping.

He never had been when she'd shown up, but they'd wasted plenty of time kissing once she arrived. A smile touched his face just thinking about that, and he couldn't wait to get this ceremony done so she could have her farm, and he could be her husband.

Maybe you did fall for her in two seconds flat, he thought.

He shook his head as Ian and Cayden finally entered the room. They came to say congratulations to Duke, though all Ian did was nod along with what Cayden said. Cayden was more dressed up than Duke, but he didn't care. It was his wedding, and as long as his bride-to-be was happy, it didn't matter what his brothers, his mother, or anyone else thought.

There wasn't going to be a traditional wedding party who marched down the aisle ahead of Lisa. Her father had passed away, and she'd asked her oldest half-brother to escort her down the aisle.

Duke was going to walk down the aisle in a crowd of his brothers, and they'd all take their seats while he stood at the altar. Then Bruce would bring Lisa to him, the ceremony would be performed, and then dinner would be served.

He could already smell the beef tenderloin, and when he and Lisa had stopped by this morning to let the party supply company in, he'd caught a whiff of chocolate cake and cheesecake. He'd ordered both for their wedding luncheon, and if there was one thing Duke was really good at, it was ordering good food.

"You're a good man, Duke," Mom said, taking his face in one of her hands. She kissed both of his cheeks. "Come on, Gus. Let's go get a seat." She ran her hands along Daddy's shoulder as she left, and they had an entire conversation with a single look.

They'd been married for over fifty years now, and Duke wondered if what he was doing today would last that long. Down inside him, he hoped so, and he thought that was part of being in love.

He'd never been in love before, so it was ground Duke hadn't trod before. Nerves ran through him, and he took a deep breath.

"Nervous?" Blaine asked, and Duke nodded. "Group hug," his brother called, and before Duke could say he didn't want that, all the Chappells, including Daddy, converged on him. They huddled up, the same way they had before Blaine's wedding, and while Duke had enjoyed the sense of brotherhood and camaraderie then, he didn't want it directed at him.

"This makes more than half of you married," Daddy said. "With three-quarters of the boys hitched by spring."

Duke kept his eyes on the ground, because he already felt enough emotion.

"I love you boys," Daddy said. "Your mother loves you. We're thrilled you've found women to love you, and we hope to stay alive long enough to see the family as it keeps growing."

"Love you, Daddy," Duke said with several of his other brothers.

Thankfully, the door opened, and Ginny said, "It's time, Cay."

"Let's go," Cayden said, and the huddle broke up. Duke let his brothers file into place around him, and he reached up to adjust his cowboy hat.

"It's okay?" he asked Cayden, who knocked it right a little bit.

"It's great."

"Let's do this," Duke said, and he took the first step toward the door. Spur led the way out, and they walked in a group without order or sequence. Down the hall and out into the living room Duke went, then he turned and went through double-wide doors to the ballroom.

Soft music played throughout the room, and the ceiling stretched two stories up. Immaculate art sat on the walls, and the grand piano welcomed him on his right. About one hundred chairs had been set up, and they were nearly all full. Her family, plus his did that job, and she'd invited a few friends of hers from the farm.

His mother had then sent out invites for as many remaining seats as Duke would give her, and he knew it was important to her to have her high society friends there. He stepped over to her and Gus, who was mesmerized by the fancy hat Mom had put on.

"Love you, Mom."

"Love you too, Dukey." Her voice broke on his child-hood nickname, and Duke pressed his cheek to hers.

He stepped over to the altar, which wasn't one of those beautiful, carved ones Tam had made with her bare hands.

Next time, Duke thought, and he hoped it would be a vow renewal ceremony and not a completely new woman and a completely different wedding where he'd get his custom-made altar.

He took a breath, held it, and turned toward the back of the ballroom. He didn't have to wait long for the women to appear, and they came down the aisle in a flock too, each branching off toward her husband and leaving his view to Lisa unobscured.

He expected to see her standing there, all dressed up, with a fancy up-do and lots of makeup on her face.

Instead, she wore a pair of blue jeans that made her legs look ten miles long, her dark blue cowgirl boots, and a blouse the color of ivory.

He started laughing, and when the sound filled the ball-room and reached Lisa's ears, she grinned and nodded at Bruce to take her down the aisle.

When she reached Duke, he took her into his arms, the two of them chuckling together. "You're so beautiful," he said. "What made you change your mind?" He brushed her loose curls back off her shoulder, realizing he could see through her blouse to a dark blue camisole underneath. She was elegant and rugged at the same time, and his soul fused to hers in a way he'd never experienced before.

"You were right," she whispered. "We aren't fancy

people, and I don't want a fancy wedding, even if the venue is really fancy."

"You do want to do this still, right?" Duke asked, his mouth barely moving.

"Yes," she said. "Yes, I want to do this."

"Great." Duke faced the pastor and took her hand in his. "Let's do this."

CHAPTER 16

Trey watched Robert Merchant walk around Perfect Strike, the horse Beth and Trey had entered in the Sweetheart Classic. Rob had been working with the dark roan for months, and Trey had high hopes for the upcoming race.

The Triple T Ranch didn't need the money in quite the same way as they had last year, but Trey wanted to win none-theless. Turned out, he possessed quite the competitive streak, and when his horses won in the amateur races, he felt equal to Ian and Conrad.

Stupid, he knew.

It did keep him leaning against the fence though, glancing up at the giant screen that showed him how long until his heat.

Thirty more minutes. He'd left Beth and TJ upstairs in the suite he'd rented, and his mother and father should be arriving any moment. He should go so he could spend some time with them before Perfect Strike took to the track.

Rob knew what he was doing, and Trey had been working with the horse at the track on the ranch for many nights. He loved working with the horse in the dark, quiet hours of the night, but he was also looking forward to getting a good night's sleep.

He knew that would only happen until Beth delivered, and she was due in only six more days. She said she'd been late with TJ, but she certainly looked ready to pop.

"All right then," Trey called, and Rob looked his way. The jockey smiled and patted Perfect Strike's flank before coming toward him.

"He's lookin' good," Rob said. "Really strong. We've done practice runs at full-out faster than what the other heats are putting up." He knocked on the metal railing. "I'm feeling good. Guess we'll see."

"Guess we'll see," Trey said. "Remember, he likes—"

"To pull left, I know." Rob grinned at Trey. "And he likes to explode out of the gate. I know how to hold him back. We've talked about his sprinting habit, he and I."

Trey chuckled with Rob, though both of them spoke to Perfect Strike as if he were a human. Trey loved telling his horses his deepest secrets and desires, because they didn't ask him questions or make him examine things he didn't want to.

"Have a good race," Trey said, and he straightened. Rob turned to go back to the holding stable, and Trey turned to merge back into the crowd. Last year, he'd been on the ground the whole time, right down until when Rob went through the gate to get to the starting stalls.

Today, though, he could relax. He could go spend time with his wife, son, and parents. He'd legally adopted TJ last fall, and they were simply waiting for the new legal documents to come through before talking to him about changing his last name.

Beth didn't necessarily want TJ to take on the name Chappell, because he had a father and a good last name. Trey wasn't sure how he felt about it. He'd be listed as the boy's father in all legal ways, and it felt a little strange for the boy to have the last name Dixon when Trey's was Chappell.

He'd do whatever Beth wanted, though, because the truth was, he hadn't fathered TJ. He was more willing to argue with her about what they'd name their daughter, and he hoped the baby would hold on for a little longer so he could bring it up with Beth again.

"Hey," he said, entering the suite. "TJ talked you into the nachos, I see." He grinned at the child, whose cheeks were stuffed full of the chips, ground beef, and cheese he loved.

"We got you a double bacon cheeseburger," Beth said, indicating the paper bag there. "Your parents are on their way in."

He leaned down and kissed her, placing one hand on her belly. "How are you?"

"Good," she said. "Stuffed after three bites, but good."

"The baby?"

"Kicking me a lot," Beth said, pressing on her left side. "She feels like she's rolling today too."

"Better than making your back ache."

She'd told him that back aches were actually good, especially this late in a pregnancy. It meant she was in the very early stages of labor, but Trey didn't see how living in constant pain and discomfort was ever good.

She flashed him a smile and nodded toward the track. "Only one race to go."

"Mm."

"You're not nervous, are you?"

"Of course I'm nervous," he said. "We won last year, and they put that ridiculous star next to our horse's name. Everyone's going to be watching him." He took a seat at the table beside her and opened his bag of food. "That means they're going to be watching us."

"We're in a booth," she said. "With tinted windows on the sides. No one's watching us."

"I had the guy in the elevator call me by my name." Trey cocked his eyebrows at her and unwrapped his cheeseburger. "They're watching."

"Let 'em watch," she said. "Maybe then they'll see that you and Rob are the best trainer-jockey pair in the state."

Trey grinned at her, because she always knew what to say to build him up, and she knew exactly what to do to make him feel like the man he wanted to be.

The announcer came over the speaker system to announce the next race, and the horses came out onto the track. It wasn't his race, but Trey felt the same quaking in his gut as if it was. He ate his hamburger and the fries and even some of TJ's nachos.

His parents arrived just as the race started, and Trey turned from the front of the suite to greet them.

"No wonder the halls were empty," Daddy said. "Race is on."

"We're next," Trey said, returning his attention to the lead horse as they started around the first turn. The race only lasted a minute or so, but it felt like a long time to Trey. Everything leading up to a race where he had such a vested interest seemed to drag on and on.

Beth's pregnancy had been nine years long, for example, not just nine months.

The door to the suite opened, and a couple of his brothers entered, engrossed in a conversation that sounded more like an argument. When Trey heard Ian's voice, he wasn't surprised. Every conversation with Ian seemed to turn into an argument.

The man was one of the saltiest humans on the earth, and if Trey just needed to rant about something, Ian was the brother he went to. He'd validate Trey no matter what, and he actually got as upset as Trey, even if he didn't care about the topic of the rant.

He and Conrad bickered constantly, like an old married couple, and Trey had spent a lot of time worried that he didn't have a partner in the family the way the two of them did. At the same time, he liked spending time with Lawrence, and even Duke now that the man had settled down a little bit. He was taking a bunch of ranch management classes, and he liked what Beth made for dinner and had been over several times in the past.

He'd sort of disappeared since starting his relationship with Lisa, and Trey made a mental note to invite Duke and Lisa over for dinner in the near future.

The race ended, and the energy in the stadium dissipated. He went back to the table, where his brothers had settled and were snacking on a couple of bags of chips. "Hey guys," he said.

"Spur and Olli are buying sandwiches," Ian said. "Lawrence and Mariah got stopped by someone who knew her, and they looked a little panicked when we went by." He grinned like that was great news, and Trey just shook his head.

Within five minutes, the suite was full to standing room only, and that was fine by Trey. He stood in the corner of the booth, near the front wall and railing, watching the far end of the track where the horses would come in.

The tractors had been grooming the track for what felt like a decade, and finally the speaker system crackled. The announcer started with the horse names, the owner, and the jockey, and when he got to Perfect Strike, he said, "Finally, from last year's winners of the Sweetheart Classic, Trey and Beth Chappell, we have Perfect Strike, ridden by Robert Merchant."

It might have been Trey's imagination, but it sure did sound like the crowd cheered louder. He watched the roan get in the starting stall, though they practiced so much without it. Rob looked bigger than the other jockeys, because he was. Perfect Strike loved him though, and if Rob could keep him from sprinting out of the gate and around the first turn, they might actually win this race.

Trey cinched his arms across his chest and tried to block out everything going on around him. Finally, the betting closed and the gates were set.

The air stilled, and then the bell rang. The horses exploded out of the gate, and the men and women in his suite started whooping as if they'd already won. He couldn't remember if he'd yelled at his horse to run faster last year or not, but this year, he did not.

Rob let a pretty gray horse pass him, and he moved over to the rail as a pure black horse and his rider took the second position.

"Perfect," Trey said under his breath, eyeing the distance to the first turn. Perfect Strike loved to pass on the corner, and Trey expected Rob to move up a position on that first turn then hold the others off while saving Perfect Strike until the last turn.

"Yes," Trey said, the word coming out as a yell as Rob did exactly as he predicted he would. Running in second on the far side of the track, Perfect Strike edged closer and closer to that gray lead horse.

"Hold him," Trey said, leaning forward to grip the railing. "Hold 'im, Rob!"

Trey had ridden a horse on the far side of the track, and he knew the jockey couldn't hear him. On that side, there was nothing but dirt, wind, and the galloping of horse's hooves. It was what peace was made of, actually.

"They're on the corner," Beth said. "Shouldn't he be letting him go?"

"He will," Trey said, the words a shout. "He's gonna let him go. Let him go!"

The gray horse came off the turn half a body in front of Perfect Strike, and Trey saw the moment Rob released his tension on the reins. Perfect Strike surged forward on the next stride, and with the second, he pulled ahead.

The suite went wild, and wow, Trey's brothers were *loud*. He whooped and encouraged his horse to run faster and faster along with everyone else, only quieting when Perfect Strike was four body lengths ahead of the gray horse.

He crossed the finish line well ahead of the other equines, and Trey turned toward Beth and lifted her right up off her feet.

"Oof, put me down, baby," she said, laughing. He did, realizing how big she was, and she made sure she was steady on her feet before he started towing her toward the door.

"Come on, Teej," he called to his son. "Owners get to go in the winners' circle, and that's us." The little boy skipped toward the door, and Trey scooped him up into his arms, happier than he'd ever been.

* * *

Only twelve hours later, Trey was awakened in the middle of the night by a shrill cry. He sat straight up, his heart pounding. "Beth?" He reached for the lamp on his side of the bed, snapping it on and flooding the room with yellow light.

Beth wasn't to his left, where she slept. The sheets and blanket had been pushed back and toward the middle of the bed, which was pretty typical for her these last couple of months. She got hot when she slept, and she needed some support on her back as she slept on her side with a very pregnant belly.

There was blood on the sheets.

Trey jumped out of bed, his pulse pounding now. "Beth," he called loudly. "Talk to me. Where are you?"

He started toward the bathroom, and he entered the room just as Beth opened the door that separated the toilet from the rest of the bathroom. She met his eye with a wild look in hers, and he remembered the very first time he'd been in this bathroom.

She'd cut her hand in the barn, and she'd come in to clean it up. The wound wouldn't stop bleeding, and Trey had taken her to the hospital, where she'd gotten a lot of stitches.

He was going to take her to the hospital again. Right now.

Go! his mind screamed at him, and he dashed toward Beth as she reached for the wall to steady herself. "Come on, sweetheart," he said, looping his arm under hers so she was hanging on his shoulders. "I'll call Lawrence, and he'll come sleep with TJ."

He swiped his phone from the nightstand and made Beth lean against the wall while he pulled on a shirt and his shoes. With their baby bag in tow, he dialed Lawrence and then got his wife moving toward the exit that led into the garage.

"Your wife better be in labor," Lawrence said crossly.

"She is," Trey said. "I'm putting her in the truck right now. Can you come be here for TJ?"

"He has school in the morning," Beth said, panting.

"We have a schedule for him, sweets," Trey said to her. "Like, right now, Lawrence?"

"I'm five minutes away. Go. He'll be fine until I get there."

Trey helped Beth into the truck, where she leaned her head back, her face white and her chest heaving. "I'm okay, baby," she said. "Let's just go."

Trey ran around the truck and got behind the wheel. He hadn't had any time to talk about her latest idea for a name, but he somehow sensed now wasn't the time. "We're going," he said, and he did his best to get her to the hospital as fast as he could.

He couldn't wait to meet his baby girl.

CHAPTER 17

L isa smelled the evidence of company at the house before she entered it. She was so done with this spring, and the splattering of mud she wore from her forehead to the tips of her boots could've told anyone that.

She was in no mood to entertain or talk that night, but one step through the back door and into the mud room told her Duke's brothers had come over. She sat down on the bench her husband had put just inside the door, and she pulled off her muddy boots. She could admit she liked having Duke around the farm.

She *really* liked it.

She liked this bench, and she liked that he got up before her and brewed the coffee. She liked that he was home in the afternoon to do his classes, and that he ordered dinner almost every single night.

He took great care of her, and when she'd complained

that she didn't have enough time to keep a house this big clean, he'd called a maid service to come in once a week.

They'd been married for almost a month now, and Lisa enjoyed nothing more than she did cuddling into the handsome, relaxed cowboy in the evenings while they watched TV. She almost always fell asleep, and he'd wake her when he picked her up and took her down the hall to her bedroom.

He'd bend over and kiss her goodnight, and he was the perfect gentleman and hadn't said a single word about his bachelor pad in the basement.

Her brothers and their wives and kids had come to the house a couple of times, and since they knew the marriage wasn't wholly authentic, she didn't worry about them going into the basement. She hadn't been down there, but Duke had admitted to putting some groceries down there, and not keeping things super neat down there.

She wasn't sure who knew what in his family, because he'd mentioned that he suspected Trey and Lawrence knew the marriage wasn't all the way up-and-up, but they'd not come out and said so.

Trey and Beth were the first people she saw when she entered the kitchen, and Beth looked so good. "Hey," she said with a smile. "Rough day out there tonight, isn't it?" She nudged Trey, who looked at Lisa.

He grinned and said, "She looks like you did an hour ago, baby." He stepped forward and gave her a quick pat on the upper arm. "Howdy, Lisa. Duke just ordered pizza, so you have time to shower."

"Perfect," Lisa said, putting a smile on her face. She did

like Trey and Beth a lot, and they'd brought their baby. Ginny currently held the tiny girl in the living room, where Duke stood when he saw her.

"Honey," he said. "Food's on the way if you want to go shower." He left Cayden, Spur, Olli, and Lawrence in the living room and came to kiss her. "How are the twins?"

"Moody," she said, and she wasn't sure if she was talking about the new foals or her own self.

Duke chuckled, the weight of his hand on her waist so comforting. "Mariah's running late, so I didn't order the pizza until just now," he said. "Take your time, okay?"

Their eyes met, and Lisa really liked that she could let him know she wasn't in the mood to be around people without having to say anything. She nodded and paused behind the couch to say hello to everyone else.

Her eyes lingered on the baby boy on Spur's lap, as he had so much more hair now and he could hold his head up without looking like a rag doll. He'd pinked up, and he sure did have his daddy's eyes and the shape of his nose.

"You can hold her," Ginny said, not looking away from the baby. A single tear slid down her face, and Lisa wondered what that was about. Crying made her uncomfortable, and she glanced at Duke for help.

He waved his hand as if an explanation couldn't be given right now, and Lisa looked back at Ginny. "I have to shower first," she said, her gaze dropping back to the perfect infant on her lap.

She did want to hold the baby. Maybe she didn't. She wasn't sure, because it felt like someone had boxed up every emotion she'd ever had, strapped it to a roller coaster car, and sent it flying around the hilliest track in the world.

She was up one moment, and down the next. She wanted to punch a hole in the wall as she inhaled, and break down into sobs as she exhaled. She hurried away from the others and into the shower, where she stood for a long time.

Too long, because Duke came into her bedroom and knocked on the wall outside the bathroom, which was connected to her room and the hall. "Just me," he said. "You okay in here? We're eating, and I just wondered if you wanted us to wait."

"Don't wait," she said, hoping the shower spray would cover the emotion in her voice. "I'll be out in a minute."

"Okay," Duke said with a heavy pillar of doubt in his voice. She waited a few more seconds, and then she turned off the shower.

She dried and deodoranted, got dressed, pulled her damp hair into a ponytail, and went down the hall in loose workout pants and bare feet.

She paused at the end of it, looking at the kitchen table, which Duke had pulled out and expanded with the leaf hidden inside it. With the bigger table, it seated eight people, and they were trying to cram in ten. Duke had somehow managed to save her a spot, and he glanced toward the hall, catching sight of her.

Worry rode in his eyes, and she hated that she'd put it there. "Hey," he said, approaching. "If you're not up to this, it's fine. I can just tell them you don't feel well." He took her by the shoulders and peered at her. "Sorry this fell on a bad night."

"It's not a bad night," Lisa said. "I like them."

"Tell me what's wrong then."

She glanced past him, not sure how to put her feelings into words. She hadn't had much experience with that, and Daddy never pushed her too hard. She worked harder when angry or upset, and eventually, the poisonous feelings that had been stabbing her went away.

"I mud wrestled with the twins is all," she said, smiling at him. "How was your test today?"

"Hard," he said. "I think I might have passed, if a couple of other people really bombed it." He grinned at her, but Lisa knew his schoolwork was a source of insecurity for him. He'd told her that he didn't feel smart enough to finish the program, and he'd said he was considering not enrolling in next term's classes.

She'd been helping him with a few things at night, and his confidence had increased.

He slung his arm around her shoulders. "I saved you a spot, and I rescued the last lava cake from Trey for you."

"Are you gonna eat this?" Trey asked in that moment, and Duke turned back to him.

"I said she was. You put that down!" Duke took her hand, and he towed her across the room to the table. "You're an animal," he said to Trey, wrenching the small box with the chocolate lava cake in it away from him. "Here you go, honey. Sit on down. What kind do you want?"

He bustled into the kitchen to take care of her, and Lisa tried to ignore the eight sets of eyes on her.

"Do you want to come get a pedicure with us?" Ginny asked, breaking the silence. "When I've been working as hard as you have, I find an hour away from everything really helps." She gave Lisa a kind smile, and Lisa's heart throbbed against the footprints of the walls she still had in place.

The women there tonight had already kicked most of them down on her wedding day. The four of them here tonight had come into the bride's room and helped her get ready. The sisters and mother she'd wished for had manifested itself in the form of four sisters-in-law. Ginny had done her makeup to perfection while Olli went through a basket of perfumes, looking for the exact right one.

Mariah had sized up the dress and the cowgirl outfit Lisa had brought, and in the end, all four of them had agreed that Lisa didn't look like herself in that stuffy dress. They'd helped her get dressed, and Beth had curled her hair and said to leave it down. It wasn't a fancy wedding that required a fancy up-do, and with their help, Lisa had been ready on time, she'd looked amazing, and she hadn't been alone.

That was the most important thing—she hadn't been alone.

"I'd like that," Lisa said, her voice quiet.

Duke returned as Ginny said, "Perfect. We'll get a time together." She turned to Mariah. "Tell us about your bear of a client."

That got Mariah talking, and the woman could charm a rock wall if she had to. Lisa marveled at women like her, and she reminded herself that Mariah was used to working with high-profile executives, in a professional office, while Lisa had literally been on her back in the mud forty-five minutes ago, looking up into the heavens as they continued to weep.

Lisa ate the pizza and salad Duke put in front of her, and by the time she'd finished, she'd laughed along with everyone else, and her mood had started up onto one of the hills of the track. She put her lava cake in the fridge to save for a midnight snack, and she set some coffee to brew before joining the others in the living room.

"Do you want to hold Fern?" Beth asked, already passing the baby girl to Lisa.

She couldn't say no now, but she hadn't held a baby in a long time. Her youngest niece was eight years old, and that was likely the last time.

"Come sit here," Trey said, vacating a spot so Lisa could sit down with the baby. She did, unable to look anywhere but at her perfectly angelic face. The baby grunted and made a sound like a kitten, snuggling further into Lisa's chest.

"I think she likes the baby," Olli said, and Lisa finally looked up. She hated it when people talked about her.

"Where's Blaine and Tam?" she asked. She didn't want to exclude anyone in the family, because she'd been on the receiving end of that not that long ago, and she knew how horrible it made a person feel.

"They had a birthing class tonight," Lawrence said.

"We're going to go," Cayden said, and Lisa watched as he and Ginny both got to their feet quite suddenly.

"I'll send a group message about the pedicures," Ginny

said, her smile strained and quivering around the edges. Lisa wasn't sure who else noticed, but she did, because she felt like she was standing on the edge of a cliff, straining and quivering to keep herself from falling off.

They left, and Spur exhaled. "Well, who wants coffee?" He got up and went into the kitchen with Lawrence.

"What's going on?" Lisa asked the others remaining in the kitchen. "I feel like I missed something."

"Ginny and Cayden are trying to adopt," Olli said, her voice shaking too. "She's unable to have children, and she wants loads of them." She gave Lisa a happy-yet-sad smile, and Lisa knew exactly how Ginny felt. She knew how Olli felt too, as she'd likely do anything to make sure her best friend was happy.

Lisa knew what it felt like to want something so desperately and be simply unable to get it. She'd tried to have the mother she wanted, and she'd never been able to have her. Over time, she'd learned that she couldn't control what her mother chose to do, nor could she make her love her the way Lisa wanted her to.

"That's too bad," Lisa said, glancing down at the baby.

"Being around babies and pregnant people is hard for her," Beth said. "She's a saint in my book. I probably wouldn't have come."

"Coffee, baby?" Trey asked, getting to his feet.

"No," she said. "The last thing I need is something else keeping me awake at night." She smiled fondly at her daughter, but she did look tired.

Duke sat where Beth had been, right next to Lisa. He

put his arm around her and peered down at the baby too. "You want some of these?" he asked, and Lisa jerked her head up to look at him so fast, she almost crashed her forehead into his.

She had no idea how to answer that. Her face heated, and she glanced around at the other people still lingering so close. She certainly didn't want to talk about having babies with Duke Chappell in front of his family.

They weren't even sleeping in the same room.

Yet, her mind whispered, but Lisa silenced it quickly, beyond relieved when the cowboys brought in the coffee, and the conversation moved on to something else. Horses. They always talked about horses, and Lisa was comfortable with that topic.

Half an hour later, everyone had gone, including the two babies, and Lisa stood on the porch, waving. Duke stood right at her side, and the moment they were alone, he turned and marched back into the house.

The door closed and everything, and Lisa turned to find him long gone. She hurried inside too, locking the door behind her. "Hey," she said when she found him in the kitchen cleaning up. "What's wrong?"

"What's wrong?" He gestured to the big mess that had been left. "How about we plan to have everyone over tonight, and you forgot? Then you stayed in the shower for literally forty minutes, Lisa. What am I supposed to tell them? I said you might be sick, and Spur actually asked me if you were pregnant. That set Ginny off, but she didn't say anything. Then they left the moment they could, and then, you don't want to talk about anything hard. Ever."

He yanked open the cupboard under the sink and started piling paper plates into it. Lisa had no idea what to say. Fire licked its way up her brainstem, though, and she saw red when she looked at Duke.

"What do you want me to do?" she asked. "I had a hard day on the ranch. I'm just supposed to let all of that go the moment I walk in?"

"I do," he said.

"Well, I'm not you." She pointed down the hall. "I stayed in the shower to take the minute I needed so I could come back out here and be nice. I didn't know about Ginny's troubles, and there's nothing we can do about them anyway. The last thing she needs is more attention drawn to her."

"Fine," Duke said, turning to the fridge to put the uneaten pizza inside.

"What hard thing was there to talk about in front of your whole family?" She took a few steps forward and put her hands on the table where they'd eaten.

"First, it wasn't my whole family," he said. "Second, we need to start talking about stuff. Long-term stuff."

"It's been a month," she said.

"I want to know if you want kids," he said. "Is that such a hard question? It's yes or no."

"No, it's not," she fired back, hating how he wouldn't slow down and stop what he was doing. He stomped all over the kitchen, tossing forks in the sink and putting trash in the can. "*Most* of your family doesn't need to know if I do or not, and the reasons why or why not. You put me on the spot."

"Heaven forbid Lisa talk about something she doesn't want to," he said, glaring at her. "Heaven forbid I bring up a simple question. All you had to do was say yes or no. Instead, you looked like I'd hit you with a hammer, and *everyone* saw that."

"Who cares what they saw?"

Duke threw down the washcloth he'd wetted to wipe the counter. "Mariah asked me if we'd be moving into the master suite at some point. I had no idea what to say. But I didn't turn into some fish, with my mouth gaping open. I said, 'I don't know when Lisa will be ready to do that,' and I let it go."

"I'm so glad you're perfect," Lisa said, the volume of her voice creeping up.

"Come on," he said. "I'm not perfect."

"I'm not a fish."

"I just want to know if you want kids," he challenged again.

Lisa felt like a prisoner inside her own mind. She gripped the back of the chair in front of her, wishing she could just say what she thought, the way he did. "I don't know," she finally shouted. "Okay? I don't know if I want kids or not. I see them, and I liked holding that baby, and I think, sure I want one of these. But at the same time, I'm drowning already." Her throat closed off, and her eyes filled with tears.

"I'd be a terrible mother, and I think, nope. I don't want to do to my child what my mother did to me. No kids."

"Lisa," he said.

"I'm so tired," she said, swiping angrily at her eyes as the tears leaked out. "I'm going to go to bed, okay?"

"Wait, wait," he said, abandoning his chores in the kitchen as he darted toward her. "We can't go to bed mad at each other."

Lisa turned her face away from him and ground her palms into her eyes. Bright bursts of light sparked behind her closed eyelids. She lowered her hands as she felt him draw closer. "I'm not mad at you, Duke."

"You'd be such a great mother," he said. "I don't understand why you think you're your mother."

"I've never had an example of a good mother," she said. "I have no idea what that looks like or sounds like or even is." She shook her head. "I can't explain it. I'm just too tired to talk about this right now."

"I'm sorry I called you a fish," he said, threading his fingers through hers. "I fielded a lot of tough questions tonight, and I felt like you'd...abandoned me."

"I didn't mean to," she whispered. "Duke, I told you before, I'm not good at this. I don't know how to talk the way you do. I don't know how to be the woman you want me to be."

"Hey," he said. "Hey, that's not fair. I've never asked you to be anyone but you."

He did, though. He just didn't realize it.

He reached up and stroked his hand down the side of

her face. "I'm falling in love with you, Lisa. All the way. I might already be there. I'm not sure, because I've never been in love before."

Terror gripped Lisa's heart, and she let it squeeze the life out of her.

Duke smiled softly at her. "Say something."

"I don't know what to say."

"Are you falling in love with me?"

How he could even speak the L-word was a mystery to her. She studied the shape of his hand in hers and nodded.

Duke chuckled. "That's all I needed to know, honey. Now, come on. Let's get you to bed."

CHAPTER 18

Duke left the rest of the chores that needed to be done in the kitchen. He closed Lisa's door behind him, having stayed in the recliner in the corner of the room until she'd fallen asleep. She'd asked him to do that previously, when she was particularly missing her father. He'd offered tonight, and she'd accepted.

He wanted to stay in the bed with her. She had a queen-sized bed, and Duke's frustration ran hot as he bypassed the still-messy kitchen and went downstairs. Lisa had jokingly called it his "married bachelor pad," but that was exactly what it was.

He hated it.

He hated living down here while she was up there. He hated making coffee twice—once for himself in the basement and then for her in the main kitchen. He glared at the coffee pot as he strode by, already pulling his shirt over his head.

Dropping it on the floor outside his bedroom, he continued inside, kicking the door closed with one booted foot. He stripped off all of his clothes except his boxer shorts and dropped to his knees beside the bed.

"What am I doing wrong?" he asked. Everything swirled and jumbled inside him, making him anxious and desperate. He told himself to breathe, and he reminded himself of how to deal with a panicked horse.

That was what he was at the moment—a panicked horse. Frantic to get out of the situation he was in when it wasn't even that bad.

Or was it?

His chest heaved as he breathed, and he ignored his phone when it rang. He wasn't even sure where it was at the moment, and the world spun so fast for a few seconds.

Finally, slow breaths and with Duke forcing himself to calm and think, he managed to come out of the spiral.

He'd told Lisa the truth upstairs. He was falling in love with her. He'd never been good alone, and he loved coming home to this house where she lived, even if she was still out on the farm when he got there. He knew he'd get to see her and talk to her every single day, and that doing so was so *easy*.

"She likes you," he said, vocalizing the thought as it entered his mind. He knew she did. He could feel it in the way she touched him, the way she kissed him, and the way they could look at one another and have an entire conversation without speaking.

He knew how she took her coffee in the morning, and he

knew that she hated winter with as much passion as he did. He knew she adored horses, and she liked things to be put away in their proper places.

She wasn't great at communicating, and she wasn't great at telling him how she felt. She didn't like people all that much, while Duke enjoyed a good get-together. She could dance fairly well, she knew all the tips and tricks for getting stubborn animals into trailers, and she didn't shy away from a challenge.

Duke got up and sat on the bed, sighing as he ran his hands through his hair. He'd dropped his jeans with his phone in the pocket somewhere, along with his cowboy hat. He stood to retrieve both items, hanging his hat on the rack beside the door and letting his jeans fall back to the floor after he got his phone.

Trey had called, and Duke simply stared at the icon on his screen indicating that he'd missed a call. Trey saw and heard more than the average brother, and Duke found himself straddling a line.

He probably needed to hear what his brother had to say, but half of him didn't want to hear it. Before he could decide if he'd ignore the call or return it, the phone rang again.

Trey's name came up, and Duke swiped on the call, now thinking there was an emergency he needed to know about. "Hey," he said. "What's goin' on?"

"He answered," Trey said, most likely talking to Beth. To Duke he said, "We're worried about you, brother."

Duke lay back on the bed and stared up at the ceiling.

"I'm okay."

"I know exactly how you are," Trey said. "And it's not okay."

"It's just a bad day," Duke said. "Everyone has bad days, right? Even married couples."

Trey chuckled and said, "Yes."

"Then I'm okay."

"Duke, I don't think you'll ever admit that you're not okay, and Beth and I want you to know that we're your safety net. You can always come to us and tell us anything. She's smarter than me, and she's a woman, so she might be able to help you understand what's goin' on in Lisa's head."

"That would be nice," Duke murmured, thinking of the mean things he'd said to her. Before his feelings had turned romantic, Duke and Lisa had argued like they had upstairs all the time. He actually liked her wit and her quick comebacks, but they'd always stayed on the business side of things.

Tonight, he'd turned them personal. *You apologized*, he told himself when the familiar guilt hit him. He was so tired of feeling guilty all the time.

"So come over for breakfast on your way to the ranch," Trey said. "We can talk."

"Only if Beth makes blue corn pancakes," Duke said. If he had to talk about his feelings, he should at least get something amazing out of it.

Trey relayed the message to Beth, and then said, "She says she can do that. She even has that peach honey you like with them."

Duke grinned, thinking that if Beth had dark hair, she'd be exactly who Duke wanted. He immediately dismissed the thought. The woman he wanted was upstairs, and it didn't matter that Lisa didn't cook.

Duke did well enough to get by, and he liked taking care of Lisa. It made him feel significant, and as the youngest brother in the family, Duke had never felt very important.

"See you tomorrow," Trey said, but Duke didn't answer. A light had gone on in his head, and he realized now why Lisa pushed all of his buttons and got him so fired up.

She didn't need him.

He wanted to be necessary to someone or something so badly, but Lisa didn't *need* him to bring her coffee in the morning. She didn't *need* him to make her dinner at night. She'd gotten along just fine without him before, and if they broke up, she probably would again.

He frowned as his fingers tightened around his phone. He imagined squeezing it hard enough to break it, and then he'd throw all the pieces against the wall.

Before he did that, Duke plugged in his device and got in bed. He snuggled down deep into the covers, because it was freezing in his bedroom in the basement. "If she doesn't need me, Lord, what am I doin' here?"

It was a very good question, and Duke didn't have an answer for it. If he posed it to Lisa, she wouldn't either, and he'd rather pretend like she needed him than know for sure that she didn't.

* * *

The next morning, Duke sat in his truck outside the white farmhouse where Trey, Beth, TJ, and Fern lived. He'd been there for ten minutes, and he was honestly surprised no one had come out onto the porch to find out why he hadn't come in yet.

Last night's rain had ebbed away, and now the sun shone. As Kentucky dried out, it turned green, and Duke did love springtime on the ranch. They had a dozen trees that bloomed pink, and he enjoyed the fragrance of them while Ian and Daddy sneezed for months.

His heart felt like a marble, but he wouldn't be able to live with himself if he'd caused Beth a whole heap of work in the kitchen for nothing. He unbuckled his seat belt and went in the house, the scent of bacon meeting his nose and buoying his spirits.

"There you are," Beth said, coming out into the living room as she wiped her hands on a towel. "I was just starting to think you'd stood me up." She gave him a warm smile, her eyes full of wisdom too. She came all the way to him and hugged him, and while she wasn't that much older than him, Duke felt like he'd finally been accepted by someone who mattered.

"I know this isn't easy," she said quietly. "I'm not going to make excuses for her. Everything you're feeling, Duke? So is she, I guarantee it. It's just as confusing and difficult for her as it is for you." She nodded and stepped back. "Okay? So don't be too hard on her, or yourself, and don't make any assumptions."

He nodded, his voice stuck inside the box in his throat.

"Come eat," she said. "Trey got called out to help with a pair of foxes that have been getting into our chickens. He and TJ will be back in a few minutes, I would think." She preceded him into the kitchen, where he found a full breakfast buffet on the kitchen counter.

"Beth," he said. "This is way too much."

"Oh, I'm just—I'm better when I'm busy." She flashed him a smile, and Duke slowed down enough to see something amiss in her too.

"What's wrong when you're not busy?" he asked, keeping his eyes on the stack of plates. He picked one up and moved over to the breakfast casserole she'd made. She'd surely been working in the kitchen for hours to have produced all of this. Bacon, sausage, breakfast casserole, orange juice, chocolate muffins—homemade—and as he stood there, she put three blue corn pancakes right on his plate.

She finally stopped moving, and Duke met her eye. "We think there might be something wrong with Fern." Beth spun away from Duke but not before he saw the pure anguish in her eyes. Her shoulders shook, and Duke set his plate down and went to his sister-in-law. He put his arm around her shoulders, and she turned into him, sobbing.

"Okay," he said quietly, the way he had to Lisa in the past. "It's okay, Beth. Shh."

"She doesn't respond the way babies should," Beth said. "We have an appointment with an infant hearing specialist next week."

"You think she might be deaf," he said. He'd only held

Fern a few times, and the baby was only three weeks old. He'd never heard her make a sound other than crying, and she'd slept most of the times he'd seen her.

"Possibly, yes," Beth said, stepping back and wiping her eyes. She took a deep breath but looked like she might crumble again at any moment. "It's okay. I can do this. It's just her hearing. It's not like she won't be able to walk or communicate. It'll just be different." Her voice broke on the last word, but she kept her tears contained in her eyes.

"It'll just be different," Duke echoed, the words taking on a whole new meaning for him. "Beth, you're a genius." He grinned and stepped over to get his plate.

"What does that mean?" Beth asked, but Trey and TJ walked in the back door, and they wore some of the mud Lisa had gotten into last night.

"Oh my word, stop," Beth said, holding up her spatula. "Stop right there. The last thing we need is mud all over the house."

Trey stopped and held out his hand to get TJ to do the same. Duke abandoned his food and went with Beth to get towels, and both Trey and TJ stripped out of their clothes right there in the kitchen.

Beth scampered down the hall to get new garments, and Duke went back to the table. As the three of them kept busy with getting dry and dressed and then their plates of breakfast, Duke thought about what Beth had said.

It'll just be different.

He wanted Lisa to love him a certain way. He wanted her

to fawn over him the way some other women had. He wanted her to flirt with him and look cute for him.

Embarrassment and shame filled him when he realized she wasn't going to do those things. Her love wasn't superficial and only skin-deep.

It was more than that, and he had to be willing to be loved the way *she* knew how to love.

He needed to talk to her and let her know that he was sorry for expecting something from her she couldn't give. He wanted her to know that he recognized what she *had* given him, and that he knew what her actions had said to him.

Down the hall, Fern started to fuss, the sound of her crying coming over a baby monitor in the kitchen. "I'll get her," Duke said, as Beth had literally just sat down with her plate of eggs and pancakes.

"Thank you, Duke." She gave him a grateful smile, and Duke left his empty plate at the table and went down the hall to the baby's room.

Fern had one tiny hand freed from the bundle she'd been swaddled in, and he smiled at her as he approached the crib. "There you are, baby," he cooed at her. "You got that hand out. Your momma wrapped you so tight."

Fern didn't respond to the sound of his voice, but as he loomed over her and she caught sight of him, her cries lessened. "Yes, you're okay," he said, reaching for her. He undid the tight swaddle and picked her up, placing her over his shoulder.

She stopped crying completely, and Duke patted her

whole body with one of his big hands. "Yes, you love Uncle Duke the best, don't you?"

He took the baby and the blanket with him down the hall, where Beth took a bottle out of the bottle warmer and handed it to him. He took a seat on the couch and offered the bottle to Fern. She definitely wanted it, and her eyes closed in bliss as she started sucking.

"Beth says you got everything ironed out already," Trey said from the table. "What does that mean?"

"I've been expecting something Lisa can't give," Duke said, looking away from Fern. "She's not going to show love the same way other women do. I know that—or I should've known that. I have to let her be her."

"Ah, so that's what you meant by 'it'll just be different'," Beth said.

"Yeah," Duke said. "You said that about Fern. I needed to realize that about how Lisa treats me. What she says. What she does."

"She's nice to you, right?" Trey asked. "She treats you right?"

"Yes," Duke said. "It just means more than even I thought it did."

"That's probably true," Beth said. "You Chappells aren't all that easy to live with."

"Are you kidding me?" Trey asked. "Out of the two of us, I'm the one who manages to get his dirty clothes in the laundry basket."

"That's not what I mean," Beth said. "You're loud.

You're opinionated. You're always right, even when you're wrong."

"I am not," Trey said, glaring at his wife.

"Not you, baby," she said. "But in general. That's how you cowboys are. You're very good at your jobs, and it makes you really confident in other areas. That's all I'm saying."

Trey grumbled something and took another bite of his breakfast. "Marriage is hard for everyone," he said in a clear, loud voice. "It's even harder when it wasn't as strong as it probably should've been to begin with."

"But you can build that strength," Beth added quickly. "You really can, Duke."

"I know," he said, though he didn't, not really. What he knew was that he needed to change how he thought about Lisa and make it align with the person he knew her to be. If he did that, he didn't think he'd ever be as frustrated as he was last night.

He stayed until Fern had finished her whole bottle and then burped. Only then did he pass the tiny girl to her mother. He hugged Beth and Trey and said, "Thank you for watching out for me."

"Anytime, brother," Trey said, and Duke left the farm-house. He had plenty of work to do that day—and three appointments starting in only ninety minutes. He could call Blaine, though, and his brother would get out the mares they'd be working with today.

First, he needed to run back to the house where he lived in the basement and make sure everything was squared away with his wife.

Chapter 19

L isa stared at the splintered wood in the field, her vision turning red with every passing second. "Stupid goats," she muttered to herself. She looked around, but she couldn't even see the beasts.

Daddy had loved the five goats they had on the ranch. He called them his kids, always with that twinkle in his eye at the ridiculous pun. He'd named them very human things like Sam and Maddy, but the names Lisa had for the rebellious goats were quite different.

She whistled through her teeth, as that sometimes called the ranch animals to her attention. Two dogs barked and came trotting around the side of one of the barns. "Come on," she called to them, and Chip and Spark ran toward her. "The goats are gone. Where'd they get to, huh? Round 'em up."

Chip cocked his head as if really trying hard to understand English.

"Goats," Lisa said. "Find them. Go. Find."

Chip barked and streaked back the way he'd come, Spark right on his heels. She had no idea if the dogs would really find the goats, but she needed to fix the fence first anyway.

"Cohen," she said when she caught sight of a cowboy leaving a barn. "Have you seen the goats?"

"Nope," he said, lifting a hammer. "Alex and I are fixing that, though. You have to be on the road with Smoking Chimney in thirty minutes." He walked toward her, Alex coming out of the barn behind him. "Harold is bringing the trailer around right now."

"All right," Lisa said, because Cohen was right. She didn't have time to fix fences and round up goats right now. During covering season, she always had two appointments per day—one in the morning and one in the afternoon. Sometimes three, if she'd overbooked herself and her studs. Daddy had driven the horses to all of the appointments, with Lisa in the shotgun seat. She'd learned from him on the drives through the Kentucky countryside, and she'd loved stopping to get a hamburger from a roadside stand on the way back to the farm.

She learned that Daddy liked to go to all the ranches where he did business, because then he got to see the people who ran them. He got to see their operations. He got to know them and become friends with them.

We own a business, Lisa, that's true. But never forget that people run their businesses too. You'll always win out if you think about the person before the business.

His words ran through her mind in their fullness now,

and part of them had prompted her to apologize to Duke all those months ago. He was a real person too, and just because he could rub her the wrong way sometimes didn't mean he didn't have feelings.

She increased her pace as she walked away from the splintered fence and toward the stable where Smoking Chimney lived. She hadn't seen Duke that morning, though the coffee had been just as hot and just as fresh as it had on other days.

He didn't always keep her up-to-date on the minute-by-minute activities of his day, but she wished she'd been able to see him. She wanted to thank him for staying with her last night, and for saying hard things to her. She'd thought about what he'd said, and while she still had more thinking to do, Duke was still the only safe place in her life.

"Morning, Harold," she said to the foreman on the ranch when she arrived outside the stable. Harold had the truck and trailer there, and he looked like he was about to open the back door. "Thanks for gettin' this goin'."

"Sure thing." He did open the back door so they could get the horse inside. "Paperwork is on the front seat. Is Rosalee going with you again?"

"I haven't asked her," Lisa said. "I can make the trip solo." She smiled at Harold, who was at least a decade older than her. He'd been working for Daddy for fifteen years now, and Lisa did like him. He was always willing to help out in a pinch, and Lisa had once slept on his couch when she was gravely ill and Daddy had been gone on an appointment.

"All the way to Lehr's?" Harold asked. "It's far, Lisa."

"Oh, is it Lehr's today?" she asked. That would actually be better, because they'd load up three studs and do all three appointments at one farm.

"Yes," Harold said. "That's why I have the triple out."

Lisa looked at the horse trailer as if she'd never seen one before. She needed to get her head back on straight, because she hated the curious look Harold gave her as he reached for a pair of reins.

"It's a three-hour drive, Lisa. You shouldn't go alone. Your daddy never went alone."

"Well, I can ask—"

"I'll go with you."

She spun toward the sound of Duke's voice, sure he wouldn't be there. She'd just hallucinated his voice, because she wanted to hear it so desperately.

He did stand there, though, dressed in his jeans, boots, cowboy hat, and a blue jacket that showed a black and white shirt underneath. "You can't go," she said. "You have your own covers today."

"Blaine's going to handle them," Duke said easily, his voice somewhat aloof. "You can't make a three-hour drive alone. I agree with Harold on this one."

Of course he did. Fire licked through Lisa, but she tamed it into tiny spurts of flame.

"Listen," Duke said. "I'm real sorry about last night." He reached her and touched her fingertips with his. "I've been a real idiot, and I'd love to go with you today so we can talk about it."

"About you being an idiot?" she asked.

He smiled at the ground, lifting his eyes to hers. "Yeah, about that."

He hadn't been the only one hurling words across the kitchen last night. "Sounds like a plan to me," she said. "Daddy and I would always get burgers on the way back from Lehr's. There's a little stand only about twenty minutes away from their ranch, and it was our reward for getting so much done in one day."

"I can go for a burger any time of day or night," Duke said.

"Don't I know it," Lisa said, taking his hands in hers fully and squeezing them. "I'm sorry too, you know."

"You have nothing to be sorry for," he said. "I'll explain in the truck." He stepped back as Harold returned with Chimney. "Who else are we taking today?"

"Runs with Scissors," Harold said. "Excuses are for Toddlers."

Duke chuckled at the names, and he and Lisa went to get the other two horses. He said he'd gone to Trey and Beth's for breakfast, and he'd got to hold his niece. "They think she might not hear real well," Duke said. "Poor Beth broke down a little. I guess they have an appointment coming up to learn more."

"That's terrible," Lisa said, her heartbeat pouncing in her chest. "I hope they can find answers."

"We should pray for them," Duke said, and Lisa liked that the man had physical *and* spiritual muscles. Her own spirit felt so tired all the time, and Lisa wondered if she'd pray more or exercise her faith more if that would improve her mental fortitude.

"That's a great idea," she said. "You get Scissors. He's down on the right, third stall."

Duke went to get the horse, and they did work together well on the farm. Her mind felt more free when she had reins in her hand, and Lisa was mostly relaxed when she got behind the wheel of the F-350.

She waved to Harold and reached to adjust the radio while Duke examined the paperwork and buckled his seatbelt. "Okay," he said with an exhale. "Three hours trapped in the cab together." He gave her a devilish smile, but Lisa's stomach actually jumped.

"Let's get the hard stuff out of the way first," she said.

"Okay," he agreed. "You go first."

She flipped the truck into gear and eased it forward, feeling the trailer move with it and hoping her studs in the back were ready for a long drive.

"I'm sorry I don't talk to you," she said. "I want to. I just don't know how."

"I don't need you to be different," he said. "That's what I realized this morning. You show you care in a completely different way than I do, but I've been expecting you to show me the way I show other people." He shook his head. "I'm the idiot. I'm sorry."

Lisa flexed her fingers on the wheel. "What do you mean?"

"I mean, well, like for example. What would you get me for my birthday?"

"That's easy," she said. "You've been complaining about your work gloves for a week. I'd get you new gloves and probably your favorite treat." Shame burned through her. "Something easy like that. One stop, because I'm busy, but I want you to know I thought about you and know what you like, and that I'm listening to you when you talk."

"Ah-ha," he said. "Exactly. You'd get me something like that because it shows me all kinds of other things."

"What would you get me?"

"I'd make sure the kitchen counter was full of flowers when you woke up in the morning," he said. "I'd be awake before you so I could tell you how amazing you are and hold you while I whisper that you're going to have the best day ever. Then I'd make sure you had the best day ever."

Lisa started laughing, because that did have Duke written all over it.

"I'd pull out all the stops," he said. "I'd say it. I'd want you to know through what I did and what I said. But mostly what I said." He turned a little bit toward her. "You'd get me a great gift and say happy birthday, honey. You'd let me kiss you, because you do like kissing me. And then you'd go about your day."

"Yeah," Lisa said slowly, because he was absolutely right. "And that's good? Or bad?"

"It's not good or bad," he said. "What's bad is me expecting you to be me. Act like me. Do what I'd do. You're not me."

"I'm not you," she said.

"I'm fine with how you show your love," he said. "Now that I know, I can see it everywhere."

Lisa swallowed, because she wasn't sure if she was in love with Duke Chappell. "Let's talk about that a little more," she said.

"Which part?"

"The love part," she said, nearly choking on the words. She could easily toss the words *love you, Daddy* over her shoulder as she went out the back door to go to work. She'd never uttered those words to a man, though.

"I am falling in love with you," he said. "I've been doing everything I can to slow myself down, because I don't want my mother to be right."

Lisa smiled and glanced at him, easing up on the accelerator as she came to a corner. She didn't need to throw them all over the cab, and she had three precious horses in the trailer behind her.

"I can feel it," he said. "I can say it."

"I can feel it," she said slowly. "I don't know how to say it."

"That's because you *show* people you love them by what you do. I can see it around the house. You clean up all my breakfast dishes. You make sure you park way over on the left side of the garage so there's room for me. You bring me my caffeinated sodas in the middle of my class, because you know I'm about to fall asleep."

He grinned at her. "You do my laundry. You're absolutely dedicated to this farm, and you're one of the hardest working women I've ever met. What you care about, you work on."

Lisa listened to him talk, trying to think it all through and decide if he was right or not. "I suppose," she finally said.

"I could be wrong," he said. "But you kiss me, and you hold my hand, and you lay in my lap while we watch movies. All of that is you *showing* me you want to be with me. You don't say it, but you definitely say it."

"I can admit that I like having you at the house," she said, swallowing again. They'd reached the highway, and Lisa didn't have much in the way of driving to distract her. "There's energy there that only another person can bring."

"Would you be happy with anyone in the house with you? Or is it me that you like?"

Lisa didn't need to think about that. "It's you, Duke. You have this magnetic personality. Don't tell me you don't know." She glanced at him, wondering if he did know or not. He'd gone out with a lot of women. What did he think drew them to him?

"Tell me more about that," he said.

"I don't know," Lisa said. "You're just...fun. You have a quick smile, and you light up the room. You're never on your phone, but you actually listen to me when I talk. You side with me when I rant about something happening out on the farm, whether I'm right or not. You tell me I'm pretty when I'm clearly a mess."

She shrugged and reached to turn the volume down on the radio. "Out of all of your brothers, you just...call to me.

I'm sure other women have felt the same way. That's why you have so many dates." She looked at him quickly and put her eyes back on the freeway. "Right?"

"I've never had anyone explain it like that," he said. "I thought it was just because of my good looks." He grinned, and Lisa actually laughed with him.

"Those only add to your charm," she said dryly. "Now you know it, so you're going to be a beast to live with."

"I am not," he said. "I'll pretend like you didn't tell me I was the most charming and most handsome man you've ever met."

"I did *not* say that," she said with a laugh, though she could've easily said that. He *was* the most charming and most handsome man she'd ever met.

He chuckled, and then he reached over and took her hand in his. He kissed the back of her palm and said, "I have one more thing I want to talk about, Lise."

Her heartbeat trembled in her chest, but if there was just one more thing, she could do it. "Okay," she said. "Shoot."

"It's about the sleeping arrangements..."

CHAPTER 20

Cayden Chappell held his wife's hand as they left the office building. He wanted to ask her what she was thinking, but Ginny wore a look on her face that said she was still processing. He held his tongue and helped her into the truck.

"Help me, Lord," he whispered into the sky as he went to get behind the wheel. "Lunch?" he asked her, and Ginny nodded.

She held her purse on her lap, her hands curled protectively around it, and Cayden tried to find a hint of her feelings on her face. She was simply blank, and he asked, "Where do you want to go?"

"I don't care," she said. "Just pick somewhere."

Cayden pulled out of the parking lot of the office building. They'd gone there to meet with an adoption case worker, and the amount of information had been overwhelming. He turned toward the all-you-can-eat buffet, because he knew Ginny loved a good salad bar and an amazing rice crispy marshmallow treat, and they had both.

"They didn't say it would be impossible to get a baby."

"She said our age would make a difference," Ginny said quietly. In the next moment, she started to cry, and Cayden absolutely could not stand to see his wife with tears leaking down her face.

"Baby," he said, reaching for her hand. "Please don't cry. She didn't say it would be impossible. She said a lot of birth mothers are okay with an older couple." He squeezed her hand. "She doesn't know anything. The next person who walks through her door could pick us."

"Or we could be on the list for a decade, and then we'll never get a baby," Ginny said, her voice high-pitched and tinny. Cayden wanted all of her dreams to come true, but he felt utterly helpless when it came to this.

"We can't worry about the what-ifs," he said, because his own longing and frustration was as real as Ginny's. "Remember, I told you I'd be okay with just us, Ginny? I really am. I know you're not, and I'm trying—"

"I am," she said, finally turning to look at him. "Cay, I'm happy with just us. You're the most important person in the world for me." Her eyes rounded. "My word. I've made getting a baby more important than you." Fresh tears filled her eyes. "I'm sorry. That's not what I meant to do."

Cayden looked away, because she'd hit the nail on the head. He'd do anything he could to make her happy, but he *had* felt inferior as they'd continued to explore options for having children. She seemed so unhappy, and there was absolutely nothing he could do to improve that. He wasn't good enough.

"Cayden," she said, a desperate plea in her voice.

"I'm okay," he said, still not sure he should look at her. He could smooth things away for clients and CEOs, but Ginny had always been able to see right into his soul.

"I am so sorry, Cay. Of course I'm happy with us."

"Are you, Ginny?" he asked, and he almost didn't want to hear the answer. The buffet came into view down the street on the right, and he changed lanes to be able to turn into the parking lot.

"Yes," she said. "Yes, I am."

Cayden turned into the lot, and he had to look right to do it. He glanced at her, but he didn't meet her eyes. He found a parking spot and eased his big truck into it. With the vehicle in park, they both sat there.

Cayden breathed in and out, found his center, and looked at his wife. "I would do anything to get you a baby," he said. "I would. It's outside of my control, though. All we can do is complete the file and pray someone chooses us."

She gazed at him with those navy eyes he'd fallen in love with. "Please forgive me. I never want you to think you're not all I need. You are. If it's just us for the rest of my life, I'll be the happiest woman on Earth."

Cayden smiled at her and reached for her hand. "I forgive you, my love." He nodded his head toward the restaurant. "I even brought you to the buffet."

A grin burst onto her face. "That's because you're the best husband in the world."

He chuckled and got out of the truck. Ginny didn't wait for him to come open her door, and he took her hand when she came around the tailgate. He pressed a kiss to her forehead and said, "I love you."

"I love you too," she said, and they went inside to have lunch.

* * *

A week passed, and then two. Cayden signed all the paperwork Ginny said he needed to. She'd done the vast majority of the work on their adoption profile, and he gave his opinion when she asked for it. He wasn't sure what else he could do, though he did spend a few seconds each morning and each night when he prayed that his wife would get the baby she wanted.

She was forty-seven years old, and their case worker, Kari, had said that most birth mothers putting babies up for adoption were in their late teens or early twenties. They viewed forty-seven-year-olds as "ancient," and some of her older couples had experienced some trouble getting chosen.

"It's not impossible," Kari had said. "We'll just make your profile look so amazing." She'd smiled through most of the meeting, but Cayden's stomach tightened just thinking about their meeting.

He didn't like seeing Ginny behind a laptop either, because he knew she'd be checking their profile views, their email, and everything else she could to find out if they'd been selected yet. She didn't hide anything from him, but she was always anxious after being on the laptop.

March seemed to be flying by, and Cayden had started prep for their second annual Summer Smash. Duke, Blaine, and Spur spent most of their time in the breeding barn in the spring, and Lawrence and Mariah's big wedding day sat only three weeks away now.

She wanted a warm, spring wedding, and Cayden had seen the plans for it a half-dozen times when he'd come in off the ranch. Lawrence did live upstairs, and it seemed like Mariah came over every single night.

Therefore, he wasn't surprised to walk into the homestead after putting in a full day's work to find Ginny standing in the kitchen, stirring something, and Lawrence and Mariah looking at a binder while they sat at the kitchen table.

"There you are," Ginny said. "He's here." She burst into tears in the next moment, and Cayden wasn't sure if he should check with Lawrence first or comfort his wife. She hadn't cried in a while—since their lunch at the buffet.

Lawrence and Mariah both got to their feet and came into the kitchen, and Cayden's confusion doubled. "What's going on?" he asked, stepping over to Ginny and taking her into his arms.

"It's all good news," Lawrence said.

"It is?"

"I'm crying because it's just a release," Ginny said, beaming up at him through her tears. "Kari called, Cay. She said she had a birth mom who wants to meet us."

Cayden searched her face, but he didn't think she'd joke about this.

"It's just a meeting," Ginny said. "And Mariah said that's good, but it doesn't mean we've been chosen."

"Dani met with her birth mom three times before she and Doug were officially chosen." Mariah glanced around the group and tucked her blonde hair behind her ear. "I didn't mean to sound negative."

"You didn't." Ginny left Cayden and hugged Mariah. "I'm glad you have some experience with this. I'd be so lost without you."

"So good news," Cayden said. "When are we meeting her?"

"Saturday," Ginny said, turning back to him. The three of them grinned at him, and Cayden wished they'd texted him the good news so he could be ready to celebrate instead of feeling only confusion.

"Our house plans were approved," Lawrence said. "They're breaking ground next weekend."

A smile filled Cayden's face. "That *is* good news," he said.

"We'll live in Mariah's rental once we're married," Lawrence said, slinging his arm around his fiancée. "Then move over there when it's finished. Either way, you two will have your house to yourselves in only a few weeks."

Cayden met Ginny's eye, and they grinned at one another. "Great," he said. "Then I can kiss my wife in the kitchen and no one will groan." He grabbed her and pulled her toward him as she squealed. He did kiss her, and Lawrence and Mariah did groan and boo at him.

He pulled away, laughing, and they all laughed with him. Cayden wasn't quite sure how the Lord worked, but he knew his prayers had been answered.

Just a little bit more, he thought.

"What's the birth mother's name?" he asked.

"Erin," Ginny said.

"Erin," Cayden repeated. *Please let Erin like us and help her feel at peace with allowing us to raise her baby.*

CHAPTER 21

Duke stirred when Lisa's alarm went off. She groaned and shifted in bed as she reached for it. She finally got it silenced, but she didn't get out of bed. Though April was almost here, and he'd moved out of the basement almost a month ago, it was still pretty dark outside in the morning—at least at the time her alarm went off.

He drifted in and out of sleep, wondering if they could just stay in bed all day. His mind seized onto the fact that today was Thursday, and she'd be bringing King Arthur to Bluegrass that morning. A small smile touched his lips, and his eyes flew open when her alarm sang again.

"Time to get up, honey," he whispered, rolling toward her.

She groaned again, but she let him wrap her in his arms. If there was anything better than waking up next to his wife, Duke didn't want to know what it was. "I'll get the coffee going," he said before placing a kiss on the corner of her eye. He moved his mouth lower and kissed her, pleased when she responded in kind.

Scratch the waking up next to her as the best part of being married. Kissing her after he woke up next to her in bed was far better.

Her phone rang, and that made Lisa yelp. "It'll be Harold," she said. "I told him to call me if I didn't text him by five-forty." She lifted her phone up and tapped to answer the call. "I'm up," she said instead of hello. "Yes, I'll be there in half an hour."

The call ended, and she let the phone fall back to the bed. Duke could think of a lot of things he wanted to do in the next thirty minutes, and none of them included her stepping into the shower or him making coffee.

He kissed her again, and she melted into his touch. "You're going to make me late," she whispered against his lips.

"Go shower then," he murmured, but she didn't move. She kissed him for another few seconds, and then she broke their connection.

"Duke," she said, her voice throaty and soft. "I love you."

He stilled, his hand on her hip and the other in her hair. A woman had never said those words to him before. He basked in them, as they were filled with warmth and light and magic.

Even better was that she'd said them out loud to him.

She'd shown him, especially over the course of the last month, but she'd never said the words.

"I love you, too," he said, wondering if they'd really taken their marriage from fake to real in only two months. Had he fallen too fast, the way he always did? He wasn't sure, and then she was kissing him again, this time without the sleepiness of before.

He didn't have anywhere to be for a while, but he didn't want to cause a problem for her. When she whispered, "Make me late, cowboy," though, Duke sure was happy to oblige.

* * *

Duke consulted his clipboard, the breeze today playing havoc with the papers. He made a note next to a couple of names, which he'd transfer to his notebook once he got back to his office. He was woefully behind on so many things, including keeping his tracking system up-to-date, and all of his school work for both of his classes.

He attended the classes live, but the reading and assignments he needed to do outside of them had fallen to the side as he'd struggled to keep up with the rigorous covering schedule he'd set for himself. Not only that, but he was married now, and Lisa had as busy of a schedule as he did. Whenever he could see her and spend time with her, he certainly wasn't focused on schoolwork.

The grumbling of a large engine met his ears, and he looked up. That should be Clifford Taylor, his last appointment for today. His toughest, too. Cliff himself was a bit of a bear to deal with, and he had less patience for horses who didn't want to mate than anyone Duke knew.

This year, Duke had matched Cliff's stud with Lady in Red, and that was probably a huge mistake. Lady was finicky to say the least, and Cliff was known for having tall, proud racehorses that acted like they'd won when they'd come in last.

He put a smile on his face anyway, because Cliff did have good stock, and Bluegrass Ranch had sold their last yearling that had come from Three Princes for three quarter of a million dollars.

The big, white truck came to a stop several feet from Duke, and he went to greet Cliff. "Good afternoon," he drawled at the man as he got out. "The drive wasn't bad, was it?"

"Nope." Cliff shook his hand and they turned toward the horse trailer.

"Blaine's got Lady in Red out already," Duke said, relieved the weather had dried out in the past couple of weeks. Lawrence and Mariah would be glad about that too, as their outdoor, springtime wedding was only nine days away now. Since Duke and Lawrence shared an office, Duke had witnessed a couple of panicked visits from Mariah, and at least twice that many phone calls where his brother had said it would all work out. They'd move the wedding indoors if they had to. Yes, he'd check the weather again.

Duke had been so glad he and Lisa had gotten engaged and then married the way they had. Everything in his life seemed to be converging, and he was glad he'd figured out how to read and interpret the things he got from Lisa.

Cliff opened the back of the horse trailer, and Three Princes marched out as if he owned the world. He was a stunning, tall, sorrel Quarter Horse, and Duke would love to buy him. "Wow, he's beautiful." He reached up to stroke his hand down the side of Three Prince's neck.

"Washed him up for today," Cliff said, beaming at the horse. "I think I'm going to retire him after this season."

"Is that right?" Duke asked, going right back to his clipboard. "Why's that?" He made that note next to Three Princes's name and looked at Cliff as he looped the reins around the horse's neck.

"He's getting older," Cliff said. "Not as valuable, and I think he'd like to retire." He smiled at the horse as if they'd had several conversations about this, and Duke only had time to return the smile before another vehicle approached.

This one was driven by Lisa, and he grinned as he turned away from his client and toward his wife. "Hey," he said approaching her. "What are you doing here?"

She finished getting out of the truck and slammed the door. "I was on my way by, so I decided to stop." She looked past him to Cliff and Three Princes. "You got Taylor?"

"Yep." Duke kissed her quickly and turned back to Cliff. "Cliff, have you met my wife, Lisa?"

"I heard you got married," Cliff said, his voice somewhat gruff now. "Howdy, ma'am." He did not seem interested in shaking her hand or engaging in small talk with her, and Duke looked between the two of them.

She said nothing, though—not that he expected her to —and Duke cleared his throat, the tension now riding the breeze enough to make Three Princes take a few steps and toss his head.

"Let's get going," Duke said. "Come with me, Cliff. We're in the breeding barn, same as always." Duke would normally offer to take the horse back to the barn himself, giving the owner a break. Cliff never took the offer, though, and he liked walking his own horses back.

"You remember Blaine," Duke said when they arrived. His brother turned and shoved his phone in his back pocket. "Blaine, Cliff Taylor and Three Princes."

"Good to see you again, sir." Blaine had a blinding smile and plenty of personality, and Duke sure was glad he was there. "Hey, Lisa."

"Howdy, Blaine."

"All right," Tam said as she came through the door. "We're all here? Ready?" She clapped together her gloved hands and smiled around at everyone. Duke liked having Tam's help, because she'd grown up around animals, and she could charm the owners if something didn't go well.

Duke's gut writhed, because he felt like this wasn't going to go well.

Cliff knew what to do, and he took Three Princes back outside and around to the door that came into the barn but kept the male and female horses separate. Lady in Red had to give Three Princes the once-over to see if she liked him before she'd allow him to cover her.

She'd been downright nasty to the last three studs Duke had booked, and thankfully, he had other mares in heat. Right now, though, if Lady rejected Three Princes, he wasn't even sure who he could bring out of the stable for the appointment.

Blaine and Tam went to bring Lady out of her stall, and she held her head up high as if she knew a male horse had come to court her.

Duke sometimes had a lot of help, and sometimes he did everything himself. Today, he took Lisa's hand and watched as the others started the delicate work of introducing the two horses.

"She seems to like him," Lisa said a moment later when Lady bared her teeth.

"Bring him around," Blaine said, because yes, Lady hadn't started kicking...yet. Cliff brought his stud around the wall separating the two horses, and Tam leaned into Lady to get her to turn. Tam was definitely thicker through the midsection, and Duke was surprised she still came to help with this. He'd told her she didn't need to, because her pregnancy was getting pretty far along

"When is she due?" Lisa asked.

"Sometime in the summer," Duke said. "End of May, maybe?" He wasn't entirely sure. He kept records of so many things, but his brother's wives due dates wasn't one of them.

"Mm." Lisa watched as the mare accepted Three Princes, and relief streamed through Duke as the job got done. He squeezed Lisa's hand and had just started to let go so he could go congratulate Cliff and walk him back to his truck when an earsplitting whinny filled the air.

Three Princes was still up on Lady's back when she reared, and Blaine yelled something. Duke shot forward, abandoning his clipboard, because Cliff had let go of Three Princes' reins.

Lady came down on her front hooves, and Three Princes stumbled as they separated. She kicked, another scream filling the air.

"Whoa, whoa," Duke said. A couple of other people shouted; horses jostled.

Finally, Cliff and Duke got Three Princes out of the barn. As he turned back to the scene, that was when he noticed Tam down on the ground, her back pressed up against the concrete wall. Tears flowed down her face, and she clutched her belly.

"Blaine," Duke barked, rushing forward once again. "Tam's hurt."

Blaine was still trying to get Lady to behave, and Duke ran in front of the horse too. "I'll take her. Give her to me. Tam's hurt!"

Blaine looked at Duke, recognition finally coming into his eyes. Duke grabbed the reins and yanked, looking right into Lady's eyes. "Whoa," he said when he wanted to scream *stop it!* at her. Why couldn't she just cooperate?

"Slow down now," he drawled, and Lady began to calm. Blaine had rushed over to Tam, but Duke didn't dare look that way. He continued to soothe the horse, finally getting her back into the stall in the breeding shed.

With her secure and safe, he took in the scene before him. Everything felt messy, and he wasn't even sure this covering would get the job done. He'd still have to pay for it, and he sighed as Blaine helped Tam to her feet.

"Is she okay?" Duke asked, striding forward. "I'm sorry, Tam. I thought things were going okay, so I stayed out of the way."

"Not your fault," she said through clenched teeth.

"I'm taking her to the hospital," Blaine said. She tried to protest, but he simply cut her off with, "Either I'm driving you or I'll call the ambulance. Remember how much you like riding in one of those?"

"Don't you dare," she hissed at him, and Duke sensed some history there. He didn't ask though, because life was simply too chaotic at the moment. He walked out of the barn with Tam and Blaine, noting that Lisa had gone too.

He found her standing with Cliff, Three Princes already back in the horse trailer. Blaine and Tam peeled off to the right to get to their vehicle, and Duke approached Lisa from behind.

"...just a few months ago," Lisa said, and she sounded nervous.

"Couldn't have been too long after Hutch, then," Cliff said, no smile in sight.

"It wasn't," Lisa said. "Things were just a little rushed, sir. It's nothing about Hutch."

Duke slowed, because he'd hear more if Lisa didn't know he was listening. He hated that, but facts were facts. Unfortunately, Cliff faced him, and he saw Duke coming. He clammed right up, reached up to touch the brim of his hat, and started to get behind the wheel.

"You'll send the payment over as usual?" he asked through the open window.

"Yes, sir," Duke said, arriving at Lisa's side. He took her hand, claiming her in front of Cliff. "Sorry about that."

"I hope it worked," Cliff said, frowning at their joined hands.

"Me too." Duke watched the man make a wide arc with his truck to turn around, and as the back of the trailer filled his vision and they drove away, he looked at Lisa. "What were you two talking about?"

She stared after the trailer too. "Nothing."

"Didn't sound like nothing," he pressed.

She finally blinked and tore her eyes from the retreating vehicles. "Well, it was nothing." She released his hand and started for her truck. "I'll see you at home."

"Lisa," he called after her, but she didn't slow down. He jogged toward her. "Wait a second." The only reason she did was because Duke beat her to her truck and pressed his hand against her door so she couldn't get in.

"Come on now," he said, panting and suddenly worried. "What was that all about? Who's Hutch?"

Lisa's eyes stormed and her jaw jumped. "You know him. Harry Taylor."

"Cliff's son?" Duke looked down the road again, but it was empty.

"We went out," Lisa said, the words clipped on the ends. "Last summer and fall."

"You did?" She had never mentioned him. In fact, she'd said she hadn't been out with anyone in a while. "You didn't say that."

"I guess," she said. "I don't know. He took me to dinner once? Maybe twice? I thought it was business, but apparently, he was interested." She sighed and reached up to pull her ponytail tighter. "I told you I was bad at dating."

That bad? Duke wondered, but he kept the words dormant. He studied her, trying to find any hint of dishonesty on her face. He couldn't, and he dropped his hand and stepped away from the truck. "All right," he said. "See you at home."

She nodded as if they were business partners and not husband and wife. She got behind the wheel and made the same wide arc Cliff had, as she also had a horse trailer hitched to the back of her truck.

Duke watched her go, his adrenaline coming down off the high too. He hated that he'd had to search for a lie on her face, and he hated that he hadn't known she'd been out with someone else not too long before she'd *married* him.

Was he being naïve? Just when he'd started to think everything was coming together, it actually felt like it could all unravel and he'd be left standing there, wondering what he'd missed and how he could've missed it.

CHAPTER 22

Lisa couldn't get her heartbeat to stop hammering against her ribs. The drive from Bluegrass to her farm took about forty minutes with a horse trailer on the truck, and that was plenty of time for her to examine all of the mistakes she'd made.

She had gone to dinner with Hutch Taylor. They'd talked studs the whole time. On the second "date," he'd actually brought his laptop and showed her how they tracked things at their farm. They'd texted a few times. That was all —at least in her mind.

When Cliff had said that Hutch had been surprised she'd gotten married, Lisa hadn't known what to say. Everyone on the other side of the equation seemed to think she and Hutch had been dating, but he hadn't even come into Lisa's mind when she'd been faced with the marriage requirement to keep her farm.

Hutch was dull and forgettable. Duke was the complete opposite of that.

"Tam," she said as she turned onto her property. She'd been so distracted by Cliff and the crying horses that she'd forgotten about Tam. She came to a stop right there on the dirt road that led down to stables and called Tam.

She didn't answer, and Lisa's guilt doubled. It quickly morphed into anger, because that seemed to be the default emotion for Lisa. All other negative emotions always boiled down into anger.

That anger drove her to get up each morning and keep working. It kept her grounded and helped her focus on the task at hand.

Tam's voicemail answered, and Lisa decided to leave a message. "Tam," she said. "It's Lisa. I'm sorry I just walked away. Are you okay? I hope you're okay." She didn't know what else to say, so she hung up and looked out the windshield. Tam had been so kind to her on her wedding day, and she'd just walked away while she cowered on the ground?

"You're a terrible person," she said to the blue sky and waving greening grasses in front of her. She lifted her foot off the brake and let the truck ease forward. Harold met her outside the stable and they got the two studs that Lisa had taken out that day back into their stalls.

He parked the truck and trailer on the side of the barn while Lisa tended to the horses. The chores around the farm never ended, and she could literally work out here until darkness fell. Since she didn't want to face Duke too soon, she did just that, her fingers aching by the time she headed for the house.

The lights blazed from the back of it, and her step grew a little heavier. She told herself that she could have hard conversations with her husband. The last one they'd had had resulted in him moving upstairs and into her bedroom. She sure did like the closeness she felt with him, and she told herself that she wanted him to be her best friend. She wanted him to know everything about her. She had nothing to be embarrassed of.

Duke was her safe place. He was the shelter from the storms of life.

"Hey," she called as she entered the house. She sat on the bench to remove her boots, the scent of...browning beef meeting her nose. Duke sometimes made dinner, but more often than not, he either ordered or brought food home. If he cooked, it was something easy and quick, and this smelled like someone had been cooking for hours.

"There you are, sweetie."

Lisa jerked her head up, stunned at the sight of her mother standing in the doorway leading to the kitchen. "Mom," she said, jumping to her feet. "What are you—what in the world?"

Panic streamed through her mind, along with dozens of questions.

"I wanted to come see how you were doin' now that your daddy's gone," she said, stepping forward and folding Lisa into an awkward hug. "The house looks good."

"How long have you been here?" Lisa asked, leaning into

the embrace. It didn't last long, and they separated.

"I got here about lunchtime," Darla said. "The office looks good, Lise. You've been working hard." She gave her a smile, but Lisa didn't return it. She'd been snooping around the house for hours.

Had she gone downstairs? Into Lisa's room?

She stepped into the kitchen, which flowed into the rest of the house, and everywhere Lisa looked, she saw evidence of Duke.

She swallowed at the spread of food on the countertop. "Wow," she said, her voice practically a croak. "You've been cooking up a storm."

"Just tryin' to stay busy until you came in off the farm," she said, cutting her a look out of the corner of her eye. "You're just like your daddy. Married to this place."

Lisa didn't know what to say. She had no patience for dealing with Darla, but she couldn't demand she leave.

"Are you seeing anyone?" Darla asked, her voice pitched up.

Before Lisa could answer and actually tell her mother that she'd gotten married a few months ago, the door opened again. "Lisa," Duke called.

She once again shot to her feet, glancing from her mother to the mudroom doorway. Duke appeared there, and time seemed to freeze. The three of them all faced one another in a triangular shape, looking from one to another.

"Duke," Lisa finally said. She moved closer to him, but not close enough to hold his hand. "I think you met my mother briefly...right?"

She wanted to pull him back outside and have a hurried, whispered conversation, but Darla would simply eavesdrop on them. She looked at him, hoping their mental communication was as good as it had been in the past.

He gave her a curt nod. "Once, when I brought you that food right after your daddy passed."

Right, yes. She hadn't seen him, but Darla had taken the cooler and sent him on his way. It had been a brief meeting to be generous.

She cleared her throat. "Darla," she said. "This is Duke."

Tension poured from him, but he stepped forward to shake her mother's hand. "Nice to formally meet you, ma'am."

"You too," Darla said. "Do you work for Lisa?" She cut a glance at Lisa that felt full of knives. "You look like a good horseman." Her eyes scanned Duke from his cowboy hat—dirty—to the tips of his boots—covered in dust and debris. He'd had a hard day at work too, Lisa knew, and she wanted nothing more but to shower and cuddle with him on the couch. They'd fall asleep in each other's arms, and everything would be right in the world.

Darla complicated everything.

"I, uh…"

Something behind Darla hissed violently, and she spun toward it. "Oh, the pasta is boiling over." She hurried over to the stove, and Lisa took the moment to look at Duke.

"You never told her," he murmured.

Lisa shook her head, and she regretted every day that had

passed since she and Duke had said I-do and she hadn't told her mother.

"Can I at least stay for dinner?" he asked. "I'm starving."

Lisa didn't know what to say. She didn't know what to do. She looked back at her mom, who turned toward them. "Did you get your farm problem solved?" she asked, as if a ten-second conversation could fix a farm problem. "We're about to eat." It was clear that Darla didn't want Duke to stay.

Duke looked at Lisa too, but her mind blanked. "You know what?" he bit out. "We did fix our farm problem. Talk to you later, Lisa." He turned and walked out the way he'd come in, and shock flowed through Lisa at his disappearance.

"Good," Darla said as if thrilled to be spending the evening with her daughter. "Give me five minutes, and this Alfredo will be ready."

"I'm going to go shower," Lisa said, because she couldn't stay in the same room as her mom right now. She needed to talk to Duke. She walked away despite her mother's protests, and she dialed Duke as she stepped into the bedroom they shared.

She closed and locked the door, thinking she needed to change all the locks in the whole house and start locking it up tight when she left in the morning. Then she wouldn't have a Darla-shaped surprise waiting for her when she came in from the farm.

"Come on," she said as Duke's line rang. His phone connected to his truck, and he always answered her calls. She paced from one side of the room to the other. He didn't answer.

She immediately called him again, and relief hit her hard in the chest when he said, "Lisa."

Fear immediately followed that relief, because he didn't sound happy.

"I'm sorry," she said. "I was on the spot, and I didn't know what to do."

"What you do, Lisa, is you tell your mother you married a man you're in love with. You *claim* me in front of her, the way I *always* claim you in front of everyone."

Lisa collapsed onto the bed, tears filling her eyes. She stared at the ground, wondering why she couldn't just be normal. She wanted to be the woman Duke needed, but she honestly wasn't sure she ever could accomplish that. He'd told her she could be herself, but every time she didn't do or say what he wanted her to, he told her exactly how she was lacking.

"I have to go," he said. "It's really dark tonight, and the wind is crazy."

"Duke," she said, but all she heard was the very final click of him ending the call. She stared at the screen, her chest heaving and collapsing every other second.

"Lisa," her mother called, actually trying the doorknob.

She jumped to her feet for the third time in fifteen minutes and darted into the bathroom. She turned on the shower, undressed, and stepped inside. At least with the water running over her, she could hide her tears among the spray.

CHAPTER 23

D uke's back ached in a way it hadn't in a while. His bed at the homestead at Bluegrass Ranch was nice and plush, just how he liked it. Lisa's bed had a pillow top pad that added four inches to the height of the mattress.

This hotel bed had nothing, and Duke groaned as he sat up. Light had started to filter through the gap in the blackout curtains, and Duke hadn't set an alarm. He hadn't expected to sleep much after driving through a fast-food restaurant for dinner, which he'd then eaten alone on a bed in this prison-cell-like room.

He wasn't sure how things had gone downhill so fast. In less than twenty-four hours, he felt like he and Lisa were now skating on thin ice. Tam had spent the night in the hospital, just for observation. The baby was okay, Blaine said, but they wanted to make sure she didn't have any internal bleeding or that she didn't go into an early labor from the blow she'd taken to her left side.

Guilt tore through Duke. He never should've allowed Tam to be out in the breeding shed, helping. He knew what Lady in Red was like, and he should've been the one holding the reins instead of Lisa's hand.

"Stupid," he said to himself as he stood. He stretched his arms above his head left and then right, trying to work the kink out of his back. He'd laid awake in bed for hours last night, thinking about Lisa. He probably shouldn't have hung up on her, not when she was actually trying to say something.

He also just needed a minute to himself. He shouldn't have to be perfect all the time either. He could get upset about things, and he could take the time he needed to cool down. He hadn't wanted to explain anything to Lawrence or Cayden, and one look from Ginny, and the whole story would come pouring out of Duke.

That might honestly be a relief. He was tired of pretending with his family, and with himself, and with Lisa. He'd thought she was the one safe place where he didn't have to pretend.

"You knew she hadn't told her mom," he told himself as he got in the weak shower spray. In the beginning, she hadn't wanted to. She claimed her mom would make the wedding all about her, and Lisa hadn't wanted her there. They hadn't discussed when she might tell her, but Duke thought when faced with her, Lisa might take his hand and say, "Mom, this is Duke Chappell. He's my husband."

He envisioned the way she'd look at him with stars in her eyes, that love he'd seen and felt from her before pouring into the air around the two of them.

She hadn't. She hadn't done anything close to that. Her mother thought he worked for the farm, for crying out loud.

Duke dressed in the same dirty clothes he'd worn the day before, and since the house where he kept all of his clothes wasn't a safe zone anymore, he simply went back to Bluegrass. He had a spare pair of jeans in the office there, and he managed to make it there without seeing anyone who might notice he wore the same clothes.

He changed into the new jeans, brushed off his cowboy hat, and searched the tiny closet there for a new jacket. That way, he could hide his shirt if he had to. He had three appointments that day, and once dressed the way he wanted to be, he headed out to the stables to get his mares.

Blaine and Tam wouldn't be helping that day, but Duke found Spur in the row house with Petals, his first horse of the day.

"Mornin'," Spur said, yawning.

"How's Gus?" Duke asked. He'd do anything to keep the conversation on someone else today.

"Good." Spur smiled the way only a father can. "Keeping us up at night, but good."

"Why's he up at night?" Duke asked. "I thought Olli had him all trained up to sleep at night."

"He's teething," Spur said. "There's slobber everywhere, and he's not happy if he doesn't have something to chew on."

"Ah, I see." Duke leaned against the stall wall. "Are you helping today?"

"Just in the morning, if that's okay," he said. "I have a meeting with our finance team this afternoon." He rolled his eyes, and Duke knew the numbers half of the ranch wasn't Spur's favorite.

"That's fine," Duke said. "Let's get Petals over to the shed. I don't think she'll have any problems." The mare was one of their more agreeable ones, and Duke should've had Tam on her instead of Lady. "How's Blaine? Have you talked to him this morning?"

"He called while I was at Mom's," Spur said. "We talked to him." He started to open the stable door. Duke stepped into the space and looped the rope around Petals's neck. They'd put a bridle on her in the shed, so they could control her better should the need arise.

Duke felt like he needed to be ready for anything, even with his calmer horses. He led the way down the aisle, Spur still giving him the update as he followed Petals.

"Tam is going home this morning. They're probably leaving about now. The doctor wants her to stay in bed for a couple more days, just to make sure some bleeding doesn't start. She's not too happy about that, but Blaine said he'll keep an eye on her."

"I feel like an idiot," Duke said. "I know what Lady's like."

"We all do," Spur said. "Tam helped with Lady last year. Don't feel bad."

Duke had really needed a soft spot to fall last night, and

he'd thought he had that with Lisa. That was the real cause of all of his doubt and unrest, and he pressed his lips together to keep from saying anything to Spur.

Unfortunately, the silence urged him to say something, and Spur asked, "How are things with you and Lisa?"

Duke didn't want to lie, but he didn't need to air all his dirty laundry either. "Honestly?" he asked. "Marriage is harder than I thought. You all make it look so easy."

Spur started to laugh, the sound growing in volume and strength with every passing second. "I've done it twice," he said. "And you're totally right. It's harder than you think it's going to be."

"I like being with her," he said. "I love going home at night to her. There's just so much...other stuff to work out." Duke honestly wasn't sure if he and Lisa *could* work out everything. He reminded himself that she was *never* going to react to a situation the way he did. She didn't think like him, and she should be allowed to be herself.

He should be her soft place to fall too.

"There always is," Spur said. "There's money, there's where to go on vacation. When to go. Then the kids come, and everything shifts again." He gave a lighthearted chuckle. "That's what I was talking about with Mom and Daddy this morning. The important thing, Duke, is that you keep working at it."

They left the row house, and the space opened up for Spur to walk next to him. He caught up to Duke and looked at him. "I've been in a marriage where one of us gave up working at being married. It ended. It takes both of you, both working at it, to make it work."

"How long can you stay if one person quits working at it?" he asked, revealing far too much. Plus, Lisa hadn't really quit working at their marriage. Duke actually wondered if she'd ever started.

That's not fair, he told himself. She'd come a long way since February when they'd gotten married. It had only been two months; he couldn't give up on her yet.

"I don't know," Spur said. "I stayed for about a year. I guess it's just about how bad it gets." He stepped in front of Duke, causing him to stop walking. "How bad is it?"

"It's not bad," Duke said. "I just..." Spur had alluded to the fact that Duke and Lisa hadn't gotten married because they'd fallen madly in love in less than a month, but Duke had never confirmed it.

The words surged forward now. "We got married so she could keep the stud farm, Spur. I liked her, sure. She liked me. We'd started seeing each other, but everything with Lisa is...slow. I'm fast; she's slow."

Spur nodded like what Duke had said made total sense, but of course it didn't. "So you were in love with her, and she said she might be able to love you."

"Something like that," Duke said. "I think she does love me, Spur. I honestly do. I just... She's maddening sometimes, that's all."

Spur grinned at him and clapped his hand on Duke's bicep. "All women are, brother. That doesn't mean she's stopped trying. It doesn't mean you should. It just means you have to figure out how to live with her when she literally can't pick up a bowl and put it in the sink." His smile widened. "Or how she can't park unless she has at least three spaces to swing through. Or that she gets lost for hours in flower fields and misses a dinner date."

Duke smiled back at him. "If those are Olli's biggest faults, I don't think you should be walking away."

"I'm not," Spur said. "It's just an adjustment, that's all. Maybe you just have to adjust. It's only been a couple of months."

Duke nodded, his mind whirring now. There wasn't anything Lisa did around the house that bothered Duke all that much. He didn't care about dirty dishes or clothes on the floor. He didn't care what they ate for dinner or what kind of coffee she bought.

He just wanted to be with her. Last night had been torture of a type Duke didn't even know existed.

Before he could hand the rope to Spur and say he had to go, an alarm went off on his phone. "Let's go," he said, pulling on the reins of his own life. He didn't have to rush off to make things right with Lisa right this second. He could get this covering done, and then he could call her.

As he washed down Petals and got her bridled, Duke started to pray that his wife would answer, and that she'd be in a better mood than he'd been in last night.

CHAPTER 24

Conrad looked right and then left, his truck poised at the end of the driveway leading back to the homestead. There were three entrances and exits at Bluegrass Ranch, and in the middle of the day, the one leading to the private residences on the ranch were the least used. Considering that he'd snuck away from his duties that day to go on a secret lunch date, Conrad had chosen this escape route for exactly that reason.

He couldn't imagine telling Ian that he'd started to see Ryanne Moon. Besides that, it wasn't even true. He wasn't seeing her. They weren't dating.

He'd finally gotten up the nerve to call her and ask her to lunch. They'd played tag with their schedules, and she'd been mysteriously silent about what she did for a living. Conrad had decided not to push the issue, because while they'd been texting for a few weeks, he could sense some tension there.

He wasn't sure why, and he knew how to use the Internet. He hated searching about the women he went out with though, because he'd done that in the past. When something had slipped out about what he'd seen online, the woman had freaked out and accused him of cyber stalking her.

He liked to think of it as being prepared for a date, but he'd stopped looking up the women he went out with nonetheless.

He didn't need to look up Ry, anyway. He'd gone out with her a few times in high school, and then summer had come. Daddy had been brutal to Conrad and Ian that summer, and they'd gone to Louisville for training with some of the top horse trainers at the time in Louisville. They'd stayed in a dorm on campus only a few blocks from Churchill Downs, and while the trainings had been jam-packed, and the days long, Conrad had enjoyed them immensely. He still used some of the techniques and tips he'd learned then in his training now.

He'd met Sylvia at the last camp, and he'd been surprised to learn she lived in Dreamsville too. She was older than him and Ryanne, and he'd been so arrogant and such a big shot as a senior, that he'd really enjoyed dating "an older woman."

His mother had not been happy, but that was only one of the first things Conrad had done to disappoint Mom.

He made the left turn onto the highway, committing to the lunch date completely. He'd even made sure to call it a date in at least three of the messages he and Ryanne had exchanged. Then there would be zero confusion about what his intent with her was.

He wanted to learn more about her. He wanted to find

out if the deep, booming heartbeat that had happened to him when he'd seen her last had infected her too. He wanted to ask her to attend Lawrence's and Mariah's wedding with him so he didn't have to go alone.

It was fairly late to ask a woman to a wedding, especially considering that Ry had taken a month to find a day she could meet him for lunch. He was going to try, though, especially if today's lunch went well.

As he drove, he cleared his throat and started to practice what he might say to her that day. His brothers thought he was oh-so-smooth with the women, but they didn't understand that he was just as nervous as they were. He simply had more experience, and he practiced more at what to say than they did.

Still, six of them had managed to find a long-term, loving spouse while he'd been focused on Appaloosas and stride lengths and races.

He pulled into the fast-casual pizza joint where they'd agreed to meet and plucked his phone from the console. He'd arrived one minute before one o'clock, and he quickly tapped to text Ryanne. *I'm here. Let me know when you are, and I'll come in.*

She didn't respond instantly, which wasn't all that unusual for her, he'd learned. The minutes continued to tick by, and Conrad's nerves and irritation grew with each time the clock's numbers changed.

When it was one-fifteen, he finally called Ryanne, his heart doing that booming thing again. This time it wasn't because it was telling him he should get to know the gorgeous creature in front of him all over again, but because he hadn't actually called a woman on the phone in a very long time.

She didn't answer, and Conrad started to think he'd been stood up. Ry wasn't a cruel person though, and Conrad had a hard time believing she would do that to him. To anyone.

He got out of the truck when his stomach growled, because he needed to eat whether that was alone or with Ryanne. One step away from the door, and it came flying open toward him.

He grunted and backed up, throwing his hands up in front of his face too.

"Oh, my goodness, I'm so sorry," a woman said. Conrad recognized the voice, but it took a moment to get his limbs back down and his eyes to focus.

"Lisa?" he asked.

"Oh, Conrad, hi." She gave him a fast smile that slipped from her face after only a moment. Her phone chimed once, twice, five, six seven times, and Conrad grinned at her.

"Wow. Someone wants to get ahold of you."

"It's probably Duke," she said, but she didn't smile when she said it. "There's zero reception in there."

Conrad's chest caved in on itself. "Really? Here?"

"Just inside," Lisa said. "It's like they built this place in the only dead zone. They have free WiFi, but the password is ridiculously long, and you have to ask for it." She glanced at her phone, a better, more genuine smile forming on her face. "Excuse me, Conrad. I have to call my husband."

Lisa carried two pizza boxes in one hand and lifted her phone to her ear with the other. She walked away from him, and Conrad faced the doors.

"No reception inside," he said. "What if she's been waiting this whole time?" He cursed himself for not wanting to enter the restaurant alone, and he practically yanked the door off the hinges he pulled so hard.

The interior of the pizza place required his eyes to adjust, and with plenty of light pouring in through the front windows, that only took a moment. Adrenaline poured through him as he scanned the tables and chairs, booths and bar, almost frantically.

If she'd come in, and he hadn't known it...

His first reaction was to call her again, but if this place didn't have reception, there would be no point. Wouldn't she have checked her phone a million times by now? Wouldn't she have noticed she had no service?

He didn't see her anyway, and Conrad turned and went back outside. He stepped away from the doors as a couple approached, his heart falling down to the bottom of his boots. He dialed Ryanne again, wondering what he'd tell Ian for why he'd left the ranch. He'd told him he wasn't feeling well and needed to run back to the house for a little bit.

Ian had been extremely involved in the training of one of their new mares, and he wouldn't leave her for hours.

"Conrad," Ryanne said through the phone, bringing him back to this smelly parking lot.

"Where in the devil are you?" he barked. "I thought we were meeting for lunch today."

"Okay, first," Ry said. "You can take the attitude down about ten notches. And second, I was just calling you. I've had a mishap with one of my suppliers, and I've been on the phone with them for an hour. I thought it would take ten minutes, and it's consumed me. I'm on my way."

Regret sliced through him. "I apologize," he said. "I… there's no reception here, and I stayed in my truck, and I thought I'd missed you."

"Nope," she said. "Can you wait fifteen more minutes?"

"Yes," he said. "I can go order if you'd like. Then it'll be ready for you when you get here."

"Good idea," she said, and she sounded very rushed. "I want the Yellow Brick Road. Thin crust, please. I'll be there soon."

"Okay," he said, and he'd barely said the second syllable in the word before Ryanne was gone.

A sigh passed through his body, taking with it some of the tension. He'd snapped at her, and he'd need to apologize again for that. Also, he didn't think this would be the relaxing, mid-week lunch he'd been hoping to experience with her. Not with her sounding as harried and frustrated as she had.

Still, it had taken almost a month to get this set up, so Conrad went back inside the pizza restaurant and got in line. If he could make things easier for her by having her food ready when she arrived, that would help with his apology.

He'd ordered, filled his drink, and sat at a table by himself, in very plain sight of the front door. Now, he just had to wait for Ryanne to show up.

CHAPTER 25

Ryanne practically ran across the parking lot, her long legs helping her eat up some of the distance. She couldn't believe she'd left Max alone to deal with Yardage, but she also didn't want to reschedule with Conrad. She'd been playing that game with him for a while now, testing him to see if he'd give up if she wasn't easy to get together with.

He hadn't quit, and that had impressed her. Stupid, she knew. Not only was she too old to be playing games with men, her crush on the handsome cowboy was off the charts. She could admit she liked being chased, and Conrad had put on the speed right when she thought he'd brake.

She opened the door and inhaled the scent of marinara sauce and red pepper flakes. Conrad rose from the table only fifteen feet away and lifted one hand.

Happiness popped through her as she strode toward him. "Hey," she said breathlessly. "I'm so sorry about this."

He slid one arm around her waist as if he touched her intimately like this day after day, and said, "Howdy, Ry. It's just fine," in that smooth, Kentucky accent that had surely won over dozens of women. "Food should be out any second."

She'd no sooner sat down than a waitress arrived with their food. She set the pizzas and bread on the table and whisked away the number, leaving Ry and Conrad at the table alone. She looked at him as he retook his seat, noting the clean bright yellow shirt and that dark, dreamy cowboy hat.

"Yellow, huh?" she asked. "I don't peg you for a man who wears yellow."

He looked down at his shirt. "No?"

Their eyes met, and Ry gave a half-shrug.

"I like bright colors," he said. "I think I own three shirts exactly like this one." He smiled, a light chuckle following that.

Ry grinned too, but she was mildly horrified by his wardrobe prospects. She told herself this was a date—he'd used that word multiple times—and not a sales pitch.

"You look great," he said. "I've never seen a shirt like that."

No, he hadn't. Ry didn't need to look down at what she had on. She knew, because she'd designed and sewed it herself. Today, she wore her vest tank, and it was constructed with dark red corduroy, and it was a straight, sleeveless piece, like a vest. There were large pockets on the front of it, with enormous wooden buttons, and the collar was a statement all its own.

"Thank you," she said. "I actually designed this piece." She did look down at it then, noting the zipper that ran up the front had edged down a little bit. She reached to pull it back up. No need to show more cleavage on a lunch date than necessary. "It's the original piece, and it's nice and comfortable."

"I can see that." He pulled his eyes back to hers after he'd watched the progress of the zipper going up. Heat filled Ry's body, because Conrad wore plenty of it in his expression. "I'm really glad I didn't miss you. I sent you a few texts and I even called. Then I ran into someone as I came in, and she said there was no service here."

"I was on the phone," she said again. "I couldn't answer right away."

"You said something about a supplier?" he prompted.

Ry lifted her water glass to her lips to give herself a moment to think. She'd already mentioned that she'd designed her own shirt. She'd dropped the word *supplier*.

"Yes," she said. "My sister and I started an online clothing store." She cleared her throat and straightened. "She handled most of the production and accounts receivable and all of that until she died. Now, I, uh, have to do all of that."

Conrad blinked rapidly. "I'm so sorry. I had no idea Andrea had died."

Ry waved her hand like her sister's death meant very little to her. Andy had been her best friend. Her business partner.

Her everything. "She had a very good business mind," Ry managed to say. "I was free to do all the designing, but now I'm just trying to keep it all together as we expand."

He reached past the pizza to take her hand in his. His fingers were long and slender, but somehow soft and tender at the same time. They were warm and they covered hers completely. "How long ago?"

"About five years now," she said. "I still have some bad days."

"I can only imagine," he said, releasing her hand and reaching for a piece of his barbecue chicken pizza. "I'm so sorry. I was in California this time five years ago. We had a horse that was running all the circuits there. My mother didn't mention it."

"We lived in Savannah at the time," Ry said. "They have a huge college of art and design there. I was taking a lot of fashion classes, and we were growing like crazy." Things had stalled for months after Andy's death, but Ry hadn't been able to walk away. If anything, continuing the clothing company she'd founded with her sister was a way to give Andy a legacy. It was a way to keep her alive.

She sighed and picked up a piece of her ham and pineapple pizza. Extra cheese, with a cream Alfredo sauce. She loved this pizza more than anything, and when Conrad had suggested it, Ry would've changed all of her appointments to make it.

"I own Andy and Ryan," she said. "We thought it was funny to use men's names that were our names too." She gave him a smile and bit into her pizza. A moan came out automatically, and she relaxed further with such good food in her mouth. She chewed, swallowed, and brushed her reddish-brown hair off her shoulders. Had she had time, she'd have curled it and put on fresh makeup. As it was, her unwashed hair hung limply down her back and her eyes wore yesterday's mascara.

"We're opening our first brick and mortar store on Saturday," she said. "You should come."

"This Saturday?" he asked, his eyebrows going up with the pitch of his voice.

"Yep." She nodded. "That's why I've been so busy." She leaned forward, a line he'd given her decades ago resounding through her head. "I'm not sure it's very smart for us to start something, Conrad. I'm going to be extraordinarily busy this summer."

If he remembered telling her the same thing almost twenty years ago, he didn't indicate it. "I'm willing to give it a try anyway," he said, shifting in his seat. "In fact, my brother is getting married next week, and I'd love it if you'd come and be my date." He added a smile to the offer, and she suspected he practiced that grin in the mirror. It lifted just right on the left side, and it showed his magnificently white teeth. Those full lips...

Ry remembered exactly how those lips felt against hers, and she found herself saying, "Okay, when's the wedding?"

"Thursday," he said. "Afternoon. They're getting married at three, with a light dinner to follow, and then a reception."

"Wow." She scanned his upper half again. "I think I can

probably make that work. You're not wearing yellow, are you?"

He chuckled again and shook his head. "It's an outdoor wedding, and Lawrence has us in navy blue suits, if you can believe that."

"Knowing what I do about Lawrence, I can," Ry said with a smile. She took another bite of pizza, this date going better than she'd anticipated, especially after his barking phone call. "I bet I have a dress in the back of my closet I can pull out."

"I bet you have a dozen," he said. "You being this big-shot fashion designer and all."

Ry nearly choked on her pizza. "What?"

He held up his phone. "I normally don't look up the women I'm interested in. I've been burned before, but when you said supplier on the phone, I wanted to know."

Ry took his phone from him, immediately recognizing the old article he'd read. "This is from ten years ago," she said. It was a good article, but it was outdated and not really true anymore. Life had taken her down a different path, and she'd never left for Europe the way she'd said she would in that text.

"It still says you're the best talent to come out of Kentucky in this generation," he said. "I can't wait to see your dress next week." He took his phone back from her and set it face-down on the table beside his pizza. "I don't want to wait that long to see you again. It's Wednesday. Dinner tomorrow? Friday? What's your schedule like?"

Insanely busy, she thought. She really shouldn't go out

with him again before the store opened. Still, she found herself saying, "I'm free for dinner on Friday."

"Perfect," he said. "I won't keep you out late so you're fresh for your grand opening on Saturday." He took a drink from his soda cup. "I'll come to that if you give me all the details."

She looked at him, and she shouldn't have been surprised by his kindness or his forthcoming nature. Conrad Chappell just said what was on his mind, no-holds-barred. The conversation moved on, and Ry thoroughly enjoyed her lunch with him. She'd always liked him though, and after he'd tossed a five-dollar bill on the table and walked her out, she had to remind herself that she couldn't fall in love with him after one date.

She'd made that mistake before.

He took her into his arms and hugged her, and the scent of his cologne, the cotton in his shirt, and the faint smell of horses threw her all the way back to her teen years. My, how she'd loved the way he smelled.

He was only bigger, and broader, and more handsome now, and when he stepped back, Ry knew she'd just given him a piece of her heart.

He already had the ones from their junior year in high school, and if she went out with him again, there'd be no going back.

"See you Friday," he said, and Ry could only nod.

On the way home, she started praying. "Is this the right thing to do? Maybe I should just focus on Andy and Ryan and forget about Conrad." He'd certainly had no problem forgetting about her.

"Guide me," she prayed. "If there's a reason I shouldn't go out with him, make Friday night's date impossible. Please." Right now, there was no reason she couldn't go out with him on Friday night, but she was going to look for every sign she could in the next two days.

CHAPTER 26

L isa pulled up to the house, her mother's rental car right where it had been when she'd left. Darla had assumed Lisa had run out of the house when Duke had called for an emergency with a horse somewhere. Lisa let Darla believe what she wanted.

After she'd spoken to Duke—a barely one-minute conversation where he'd asked if he could come over to the farm for lunch before he'd been called back to his work by his oldest brother—Lisa had left the farm.

Just left it, something she'd never really done in the middle of the day before.

She'd gone to Duke's favorite pizza place, and she'd gotten the pie he liked best. She didn't have Conrad Chappell's number, so she couldn't text him and tell him not to say he'd run into Lisa leaving Sauced.

Without hesitating, the moment she flipped the truck into park, she reached for the two pizzas she'd picked up and headed for the house. Darla didn't particularly like pizza, and Lisa felt slightly vindictive as she thought that was probably part of why she'd chosen it in the first place.

"I'm back," she called as she entered the house. Darla had been hard at work, spraying something that smelled like daisies and dung at the same time. Lisa found her in the living room, straightening the pillows. "You don't need to clean the house."

Their eyes met, and Darla straightened. "You shouldn't have run out like that."

"I needed lunch," Lisa said as she continued into the kitchen. "The house is just going to get messed up again. We go around and clean it up on Sunday, after church." Lisa heard herself slip and use the word "we," but she didn't care. She was going to come clean about her and Duke. She needed to claim him in front of Darla—in front of the world.

"How long are you planning to stay?" Lisa asked. "Bruce usually comes by about this time of the week, and he won't be thrilled to see you here." She glanced at her mom and then turned to get down a few plates.

"Does he still work around here then?" Darla asked, bypassing the dining room table.

"Yes," Lisa said. "It was part of Daddy's will."

"What else was part of the will?" Darla sat at the bar, and when Lisa turned to put down the plates, she found the interest plain to see. The real reason her mother had shown up was suddenly clear.

"Mama," she said. "If your ex-husband wanted you to

see or know anything about the will, his lawyer would've called you." She cocked her eyebrows at her mom, telling her to drop this.

Someone knocked on the back door, and Lisa spun that way. "Duke," she said under her breath. Mama had always been an eagle eye and possessed ears that could hear whispers through doors. She repeated Duke's name with plenty of confusion in her voice, but Lisa had already gone into the mudroom.

Duke opened the door just as she reached for the handle, and she jumped back. "Oh," she said.

"Sorry," he said.

She watched him take the final step into the house, and with her whole heart bouncing like a big rubber ball in a windstorm, she threw herself into his arms. He barely had time to catch her, and he grunted and stumbled backward a step or two with her added weight.

"I'm so sorry," she said. "Last night was terrible without you, and waking up alone is a horrible way to start the day." She pressed her lips to his cheek, then his neck, then his ear. She whispered, "Please, *please* forgive me. Please, *please* come back to the house tonight."

Duke put his arms around her and chuckled. "Sounds like someone missed me."

"I missed you," she said, the words barely leaving her mouth properly. She didn't talk about things like this. "I love you, Duke, and we belong together."

"Your mother is watching," he murmured, and she knew why he hadn't relaxed into her embrace.

Lisa stepped back and threaded her fingers through Duke's. "You ready for this?"

"Meeting your mother? Piece of cake," he said.

Not that, she thought, but she turned and faced Darla too. Lisa went out into the kitchen with Duke's hand in hers, and she went to stand behind the pizza boxes. "Okay, I got the Whiskey Barrel, because I know you like that one with all the caramelized onions." She beamed up at Duke. "This other one is called the Oceanfront View. It's more...veggie than you'll like." She glanced at Darla. "Mama might like it, though."

Darla needed to stick her ogling eyes back inside her head first, and Lisa very nearly started laughing. "Do you want a piece, Mama?" she asked.

"Just a small one," she said, returning to the barstool she'd vacated a moment ago. "I take it you two are dating. Do you think that's wise to date one of your employees?"

Lisa blinked at her, wishing with the energy of her soul that she'd gotten the mouthy genes Mama clearly possessed. Instead, she'd gotten the tongue-tied version of that, which had definitely come from her daddy.

"Actually, Mama," Lisa said. "Your assumptions are once again incorrect." She reached for Duke's hand, and his was right there, waiting for her. "Duke doesn't work for me. He owns and operates a very successful horse ranch a little north and a little west of here. I'm surprised you don't recognize him from the billboard on the way into town. He's on it with his seven brothers."

"I'm way in the back, so it's not surprising that you

didn't..." He trailed off and nodded at Lisa to continue. "Not important. Go on."

"Second, we're not dating," she said. "We're married. He's my husband, and I love him."

Darla gasped, her eyes flying open another couple of degrees.

Lisa looked up at Duke, the bright, shining love and hope in his expression worth any amount of money and any uncomfortable conversations. "I love you," she said. "I'm sorry for not saying all of this last night, but you know how I am. I just need more time to get better at it. Please, Duke, give us more time."

"You can take all the time you want, honey," he said, and he leaned down and kissed her, right there in front of her mother. He kept it chaste at first, quickly accelerating things within the kiss.

"My goodness," Darla said, and when Lisa pulled away and opened her eyes, she found Mama pressing both hands against her heartbeat.

"This is *our* house now," Lisa said. "You can't just walk in whenever you want, Darla. You should call and ask me what my schedule is. You should *ask* if you can stay here."

"We're really quite busy right now too," Duke added. "I'm afraid it's not the best time for a visit."

"Right," Lisa said. "I had to give all three of my appointments to Harold today, which means I have to go do his full day of chores in only half a day." She looked from Duke to her mama. "Daddy's gone, Mama. There's nothing for you here, because you walked away from all of it twenty years ago."

"There's you," she said.

"You left me here," Lisa said, finally letting out the hurt, the bitterness, and the pain. "You left me here, Darla, without so much as a word as to when you'd be back."

"You loved this farm," she said. "I could've never dragged you from it."

"You were my *mother*," Lisa said. "I loved you more than a farm, until you showed me that you loved your boyfriend more than me and Daddy." Anger shook inside her, but she took a deep, calming breath. The weight and warmth of Duke's hand in hers helped a whole lot to keep her steady and anchored.

"Daddy and I became best friends, and I would've *never* walked away from someone I loved like that." Lisa released Duke's hand and handed him a plate. "Let's eat, baby. I'm starving, because I didn't get breakfast this morning."

"The hotel where I stayed had complimentary breakfast," he said. "We can stay there tonight if you want."

"Great idea," she said, glancing at Darla. "That will give Mama a chance to get packed up and out by tomorrow morning." Lisa and Duke hadn't planned any of this, and she watched as the turmoil rolled across her mother's face. "Mama, why are you here?"

She didn't want to spend time with her mother. She usually had to build up her reserves of patience and kindness. Then she could see her for as long as it took to eat lunch in a nice restaurant. Two or three hours, tops.

"James and I are getting a divorce," Darla said. "I don't really have anywhere to go."

"She can stay in the basement for a while," Duke said quietly.

He had no idea what he was saying. "No," Lisa said. "I don't think that's very wise. She just needs to find a house or something. Are you going to come back to Dreamsville? Don't you have a job in Georgia?"

"I can work from anywhere," Darla said, and Lisa wondered what else she could throw at her to get her to leave. Five years was a long time not to talk to someone and then show up as if they had a relationship. Lisa could barely talk to the man she'd been living with for two months, and there were simply barriers between her and Darla that would take a while to break down.

"Honey," Duke said, his voice making the two-syllable word into three. "You're choking that pizza." He took her plate and nodded toward the table. "Go sit down and relax."

Lisa looked at him, her mind barely working. "She can't stay here, Duke."

"We'll figure something out," he said easily. "Now go on."

Lisa moved to sit at the table, and he brought her a bottle of lemonade sweet tea from the fridge and a plate of her mostly-veggie pizza. He joined her a moment later with the box of Whiskey Barrel pizza.

"Here's an idea," he said. "Ginny has this whole huge house, you know? Where we were married?"

"I'm aware of it," Lisa said dryly. "You think she'll let my mother stay there?"

"Why not?" Duke asked. "She's not using it. No one uses it. She's the nicest person ever, and I can just ask her. See what she says." He shrugged and plucked a slice of pizza from his box.

"I guess you can ask her," Lisa said, glancing at her mother. "Mama, you should have a plan for what you're going to do. You can't live in someone else's house forever."

"I know," she said. "I just need a little bit of help while I get back on my feet." She picked up a plate and put a single slice of pizza on it. She joined Lisa and Duke at the table. "I don't know why I can't get a marriage to work." She looked back and forth between them. "I wish you the best of luck. Really."

"Thank you," Duke said with a wide smile. Lisa was less inclined to grin quite so enthusiastically, because she knew exactly why her mother couldn't get a marriage to work. She had a wandering eye, number one. She was forever looking for something better on the other side of the fence.

Number two, she was selfish, with walls towering up to the sky. Anyone who wanted to get close to her had to kick so dang hard, and Lisa had grown tired of trying after a very short time. She knew she had that tendency too, and she wanted to keep her walls and fences as scalable as possible.

One look across the table, and she saw her partner. She saw the man who would help her kick down the walls and keep them low. She saw her husband, the man she loved.

"Can we go for a walk?" she asked, getting to her feet.

"Right now?" Duke asked.

"Yep." Lisa left her plate on the table, only a few bites of her pizza gone. "I just want to talk to you for a few minutes."

"All right." Duke left his pizza box behind, and Lisa had her jacket on by the time he joined her in the mudroom. "It's pretty warm tonight."

"Mm." Lisa reached for the doorknob and opened the door. The deck outside the back door stretched for several feet, and she crossed it quickly. The back yard held a shed in the corner of it, and she wanted to break into a run to reach it.

"What's goin' on?" Duke asked. "I know you don't get along with your mom, but she needs help. Are you upset I said she could stay?"

"No," Lisa said.

"Why are you running?" He jogged to catch up to her. He made it in front of her and turned around backward. "Lisa."

She reached for his hand and squeezed it, wishing she could say how badly she wanted to kiss him. They finally made it across the lawn and to the shed, and she rounded the corner and pressed him against it. "I love you, Duke Chappell." Due to her march, her breath already came in slightly heavy.

"I love you too," he said.

"I don't want my mother to stay," she whispered, her eyes dropping to his mouth. "I want to kiss you in the house, whenever I want."

"Ah, I see what's happening here," he said, sounding a bit swaggery.

"Mm, I was going to kiss you, but you just sounded like a player, and that doesn't work for me."

Duke put both hands on her waist and brought her closer to him. "Not a player," he said, his voice much softer. "We really can stay at a hotel for a little bit. I have plenty of money."

"Is that right?" She ran her hands up the outside of his arms and along the curve of his ears. He shivered and closed his eyes. "How much money, Mister Chappell?" Lisa had never considered herself a very sexy woman, but she reminded herself that Duke thought she was.

"A lot," he said, his voice choked. "We all inherited a few billion dollars when Daddy retired."

Lisa froze, sure she'd heard him wrong. "Duke." She pressed against his chest as the brim of his cowboy hat touched her forehead, blocking his progress. "Billions?"

He couldn't actually back up as he had nowhere to go, and he reached up and removed his cowboy hat. "Billions, baby. All of us Chappells are billionaires."

"That would've been good to know sooner," she said.

He opened his eyes and looked at her. "Really?"

She grinned at him and slid her hands up the sides of his face. "You didn't shave this morning."

"I'm wearing the same shirt and socks as yesterday too," he said. "All my stuff is here."

"I ran back here to kiss you," she said. "Then I think we

should take the rest of the day off and go somewhere fun together."

"What do you have in mind?" he asked, tracing his nose down the side of her face.

"I don't know," she said. "You're the fun one between the two of us."

"I'll think of something," he said, and then he finally kissed her. Because they were alone, he didn't have to keep it chaste, and Lisa went wherever he wanted to go with the kiss.

He pulled away far too soon for her liking, and she tucked herself against his chest. "Do you want to do a little vow renewal or something?" he asked, stroking her hair.

She loved that, because the gentle stroke of his fingers made her feel so cherished. He was her safe place, and the warmth whenever her life grew too cold.

"I'm actually happy with what our wedding was," she said. "You?"

"I'd like to go on a honeymoon," he said.

"I'd be on board with that," she said.

"Ideas for where to go?"

"Daddy and I usually only traveled for the studs," she said. "It might be nice to get out of the country. Somewhere warm? The beach? A cruise?"

"I'll call a friend of my mom's," he said. "He does packages to places like Cancun and Hawaii."

"You'll take care of it," Lisa said, smiling at him. "I like how you take care of *me*."

Duke grinned back at her. "I like it too," he said. "That's what I do for the woman I love."

"I love you too," she said, and she stretched up to kiss him again.

* * *

Keep reading for a bonus sneak peek of the next book in the Bluegrass Ranch series, *SAVING THE COWBOY BILLIONAIRE.* **Now available in paperback.**

Sneak Peek! Chapter One - Saving the Cowboy Billionaire

Conrad Chappell stared at his phone, willing a whole slew of texts to come pouring in. At this point, he didn't even care who they were from. He simply needed something to distract him from the frilly music piping across the whole ranch, the general excitement hanging in the air, and the suffocating tie around his neck.

Wedding number six.

Conrad loathed weddings as a general rule, mostly because they reminded him that he wasn't as happy as he pretended to be. For a while there, he thought he and Ian would live out their bachelor lives in bliss. They shared a house—a big one too—and they got along great.

Ian cooked. Conrad did dishes. Ian put in the laundry. Conrad moved it to the dryer. They'd worked together for decades, attending the same trainings and workshops, and they'd learned horse racing and equine training from their father, who'd been one of the best in the business.

Now, Bluegrass Ranch was one of the best in the business. They produced top-quality racehorses year after year. Every brother in the family had a job to do, and each one was vital to the success of the ranch.

He and Ian, though, had often thought their jobs were the *most* important. They trained the racehorses. The ones that won millions of dollars and then became assets to the ranch. They could then sell the stud fees, something Duke and Blaine handled.

Conrad had been learning over the course of the past few months that a racehorse would never keep him warm at night. He might be able to tell them secrets, but they never talked back. A horse never asked him how his day was, and a horse had never offered to bring him dinner when he wasn't feeling well.

He loved his job, but it didn't love him back. He wanted more. He wanted someone's hand to hold, a woman to talk to, and Ryanne's pretty face to light up when he walked in the door after a long day's work.

He looked up as boots came up the steps. "There you are," Ian said. "I figured you be up here." He took in the state of Conrad on the small couch at the top of the steps. They had a little landing here, and it was the perfect size for a loveseat and a tiny end table. Conrad loved to lie on the couch and read a fantasy novel in his spare time. Ian never touched it, as far as Conrad knew at least.

"Do we have to go?" Conrad asked.

"It's Lawrence, so yes," Ian said. "You usually love weddings."

"I do not," Conrad said.

"Sure you do. You find the prettiest girl, you flirt with her, and she comes to sit by you."

"Mm." He wouldn't be doing that this afternoon, though he supposed he had done something exactly like what Ian had described at other weddings.

"You're really hung up on this mystery woman."

"I am not," Conrad said, but the words held little power behind them. He hadn't told Ian who he'd gone to lunch with last week. Ian would know Ryanne Moon, as they'd all grown up together in Dreamsville, and for some reason, Conrad wanted her all to himself for a little while longer.

She's not yours at all, he thought. That was the whole truth and nothing but the truth. They'd gone to lunch together last week, with another date planned for Friday. One date didn't mean they were a couple, and Conrad knew enough about Ry to know she wouldn't want to be claimed even if they were.

She'd canceled on him on Friday morning, claiming she simply had too much to do to get ready for the grand opening of her first physical store for her clothing brand, Andy and Ryan.

Conrad had gone to the grand opening, but Ry hadn't had more than four seconds for him. He wasn't even sure they'd made full eye contact in the hour he'd hovered near or inside the building.

She'd rented a decently-sized space on the end of a strip mall that had a nail salon, a popular Mexican restaurant, a cell phone store, and a mailbox office. She'd had a lot of people at the grand opening, and she'd been busier than a bee, flitting here and there and everywhere to keep customers happy and make sure her employees knew what they were doing. He'd finally left without truly speaking to her at all, a ball of nerves stuffed somewhere in his chest.

Conrad looked back at his phone again. He and Ry had texted several times over the past week—about what they'd done for a month before he'd finally gotten a date and time lined up where they could meet.

Her last text to him had come in last night, right when Conrad was settling down to sleep. *I'm so sorry to do this*, it had said. *But I can't come to the wedding tomorrow. Something's come up, and I need to take care of it.*

He'd asked her what could've possibly come up. She hadn't answered.

Conrad flipped his phone over and Ian settled on the top step. "You know," his brother said. "You don't have to pretend not to like her for me."

Conrad looked at Ian, but he had his head bent toward the floor. The brim of his hat concealed his face. "I know," Conrad said, but he wasn't sure he did. Ian had a major aversion to women, and it didn't matter if they were nice, smart, kind, beautiful, hard-working, and nothing like his ex-wife.

To him, every woman was Minnie. Though they'd been divorced for a while now, Ian had not even so much as flirted with another woman. Conrad was impressed by his brother's blinders, as he didn't even seem to notice when there were humans of the opposite sex around.

"I'm okay," Ian said. "With whatever you choose,

Conrad. I've had some time to get used to the fact that my brothers are going to get married, whether I think it's stupid or not."

"You like Olli and Ginny," Conrad said weakly. "Lisa's great too. Tam constructed the best saddle you've ever sat in." He cleared his throat, because he really loved all of his sisters-in-law. "Beth feeds you every time you show up at her house, no matter what time of day or night it is. And Mariah actually made you laugh over the weekend."

Ian looked up, a smile on his face. "I know. I told you, I'm fine. I've made my own choices, and you should get to make yours. So just *call* this woman already. I *hate* it when you grump around the house, slamming cupboards and growling about how I've drunk all the cream."

Maybe Conrad had done that this morning. "I ordered more cream," he said.

Ian grinned at him, and Conrad couldn't stay mad at him for more than two seconds. He'd never been able to. As one of the younger brothers, he spent most of his childhood years with Duke, who was just younger than him, and Ian, who was just older. The three of them had been a real "troublesome trio," if anyone asked their mother, and Conrad was glad he still had both of them to talk to.

"It's...I went out with Ryanne Moon last week," Conrad said. "You know, the girl I took to my junior prom?"

Ian's eyes widened for a moment, and then he whistled through his teeth. "Wow, Conrad. Goin' back to your roots?"

Conrad lifted one shoulder in a semi-shrug. "I don't

know. It took over a month to even set up that date. She canceled on me for Friday, and then again last night for the wedding." He didn't want to say the next thought in his mind, but someone needed to. "Makes me think she's just not that into me."

At least, not the way he was into her. She'd consumed him, and Conrad thought only of food, horses, and Ryanne, and not always in that order.

"What did she say about today?" Ian asked. "Bringing a woman to a family wedding is a big deal, Con. Maybe she realizes that when you don't. Maybe she didn't want the pressure."

Conrad nodded and flipped his phone over again. He looked up and past his brother on the steps, to the big windows that filled the front of the house. They always cast sunlight on this couch, which was another reason he liked it.

Ian's phone sounded half a second before Conrad's. "That'll be Spur," Ian said, but neither of them moved.

"She said something had come up that she needed to take care of." Conrad tapped on his phone to wake it, and he navigated to her text. He handed the device to Ian. "That's it."

"Then she didn't answer." Ian handed the phone back. "She just opened a brand-new store. Maybe something really did come up."

"Maybe," Conrad said, but something felt false in her words. He wasn't sure what.

"After the wedding, go down to the store," Ian said. "Just ask her point blank: Are you interested in me or not?"

She'd already told him she'd be extraordinarily busy, and he'd thought that would be okay. Deep down, though, he wasn't okay with setting up dates and then getting canceled on. Maybe every once in a while, sure. Things happened. People got busy.

Ian's phone rang, and he cursed under his breath as he stood up. "No, Spur," he said in an acidic tone. "I haven't left the state. We're on our way." He started down the steps, and Conrad better get going if he wanted to ride around the ranch with Ian.

Since he didn't want to show up to the wedding alone, he got to his feet with a sigh and followed his brother down-stairs. The weather had cooperated, and Conrad was glad he'd stop getting texts from his mother about how they all needed to pray harder that Mother Nature would curb the winds.

Pray for this, Mom always said. *Pray for that.*

Growing up, Conrad had done it. He did love the Lord, and he went to church every week. He just wasn't as convinced as his mother that prayer was all that powerful. God already knew what Conrad wanted; why did he have to ask for it?

Sometimes, he didn't get what he prayed for, and he had no idea what that meant. Did God not hear him? Did he not care about what Conrad wanted?

In Conrad's mind, it was simply a whole lot easier to be the best man he could be and let God take care of the rest. If he didn't pray for something, then he didn't have to worry if he didn't get it.

Ian drove the two of them from the house where they lived in the corner of the ranch toward the epicenter, where the homestead stood. With Lawrence getting married, and Duke already with the knot tied, only Cayden and Ginny would be living in the homestead. It was still the central gathering place for all the cowboys, cowgirls, and family on the ranch, and Conrad was glad he wasn't the one maintaining it.

There was no one better for that job than Cayden and Ginny, as evidenced by the huge hanging flower baskets that had been added to the porch since the last time Conrad had been here—which was yesterday afternoon.

Someone—probably Ginny—had hung a huge banner along the rooftop above the garage that read *Congratulations Lawrence and Mariah*, and Conrad could hear the music coming from inside the house the moment he got out of the truck.

If Ian could go inside, so could Conrad. Ian didn't even break stride, so Conrad squared his shoulders and put on his brave face too. They entered the house through the garage, and despite the noise, Spur appeared at the end of the hall immediately.

"You're here," he said, stating the obvious.

"Yes, *Mother*," Ian said. "And if you'll look at the clock, we're not even late."

Spur didn't even flinch at the hardness in Ian's voice. He just grabbed him in a hug and said, "I know this is hard for you. Thank you for coming anyway."

Ian hugged Spur back, and the two of them clung to one another in such a way that revealed to Conrad how very hard it was for Ian to be here. He'd done it, though, and he was such a good example to Conrad.

"Ginny's got a whole feast for us," Spur said. "We didn't want you to miss it." He released Ian and stepped past him to hug Conrad. "How you doin', brother?"

"Good enough," Conrad said, embracing his brother back. They all wore identical suits in navy blue, but no one looked as good as Spur. No one was ever as good as Spur at anything. The man exuded confidence, and he did have a lot of natural talent with horses, ranching, and people. What he wasn't good at, he could spot in others, and he made sure they were in charge of that around the ranch.

"Come eat," Spur said. "I managed to beat Duke away from taking seconds until you two got here."

Ian had already moved into the kitchen, but Conrad's chest pinched a little bit. They couldn't even wait until everyone had arrived to eat? How hard would that have been? Ginny had texted and said eleven-thirty for lunch, and as Conrad looked at the microwave above the stove, the numbers ticked to eleven-thirty.

His annoyance surged, but he tamped it down. He had plenty of experience doing that, and he knew eventually it would go away. That, or he'd go out on the deck and jump rope until all of the negative feelings inside him swirled away. Another activity that drove his irritation into the ground was chopping wood.

Since he and Ian lived in a house with a wood-burning stove, there was always the need for more wood. With summer only a month away, though, Ian would know why Conrad was out at the woodpile.

He told himself it didn't matter, because Ian let Conrad do what Conrad needed to do to feel better. They'd always done that for each other, and Conrad had endured plenty of Ian's ranting sessions, especially when Spur had gotten engaged and Trey had gotten married without telling anyone in the family.

Conrad filled a plate with food, and he enjoyed the company of his large and growing family. All too soon, it was time to take everything outdoors, where the men and women split up into separate tents to finish getting ready.

He'd never really understood the point of having separate rooms for the bride and groom, but everyone seemed to do it. He just wanted to wake up in the morning on his wedding day, get dressed, and pick up his bride-to-be. They'd get to the venue together, and they'd walk down the aisle together. She didn't need to be *given* to him. She'd be a strong, capable woman, and she'd *choose* to be with him, the way he'd choose to be with her.

Annoyingly, Ryanne's face filled his mind. She did have beautiful, brown eyes, with all that reddish-brown hair that he loved. He couldn't quite remember what it was like to kiss her, as he'd been out with a lot of other women in the past twenty years. He kissed almost everyone he went out with, because kissing was fun, and Conrad had previously dated for fun.

He wanted to have fun now too, but he wanted to be more serious as well.

Finally, the wedding started, and Conrad got in line. He hated lines; he hated suits; he hated weddings.

He put a smile on his face, because this was his brother, and he loved Lawrence. Mariah was the perfect complement to him, as he was quiet and she was literally the most personable and bubbly person Conrad had ever met.

She was blonde and pretty, and she was quick on her feet and super organized. She'd been one of the top marketers at her firm, but she'd left to become an event planner.

The moment he stepped out of the men's tent, Conrad could see how she'd excel in such a job. Not a single detail sat out of place in the large tent where hundreds of guests had arrived to witness the wedding.

Every chair had a light pink bow tied around it, and they all looked exactly the same, the tails of them billowing in the slight breeze blowing through the tent. Lights hung in the rafters, making the atmosphere magical. Pots overflowing with flowers hung from every post on the outer edges of the tent, and Mariah had put what looked like vintage street lamps down the center of it too. They marked the aisle, and they also held beautiful, fragrant flowers.

Conrad did his part by walking down the aisle to the altar, which was a trough from right here on the ranch that had been filled to overflowing with flowers. Roses, daisies, lilies, orchids, and every other type of flower imaginable. Flowers and more flowers.

Lawrence had said Mariah wanted flowers, and wow, she'd gotten them.

He took his spot on the left side of the altar facing the crowd, where he'd stay for the duration of the ceremony. Behind him, on the other side of the flimsy tent flap, another tent waited with tables and chairs for the dinner that would be served.

Conrad could smell the steak and salt, and his stomach grumbled at him, though he'd eaten only three hours ago.

Lawrence took his place at the altar, and he turned toward the back of the tent right as Mariah and her father stepped into view. She wore a gorgeous, lace-covered gown that accentuated her slim waist and all her curves.

The very air held its breath as she made the journey toward Lawrence. Conrad watched his brother as he took Mariah from her dad, and the happiness in Lawrence's eyes knew no limits.

He wanted that, and he swallowed hard against the rising jealousy. Just another reason he hated weddings. So many reminders of what he lacked, what he was faking about, and what he wanted but didn't have.

He may have zoned out during the pastor's speech, because he blinked rapidly when the people in the tent started clapping and cheering. He saw Lawrence kissing Mariah, and he saw them turn toward the crowd, their hands clasped as he lifted them skyward.

Conrad got himself in gear and clapped for the happy couple, even going so far as to whistle and catcall as they made their way back down the aisle.

The excitement and adrenaline subsided quickly, and guests started to file into the aisles. Mom always had a crowd around her, and Conrad turned away from that whole scene.

He just needed somewhere quiet to be until it was time for their early dinner. He'd be wearing his suit for the duration of that afternoon and evening's events, but all the women needed time to change into their party dresses for the dance and reception. That would be after the dinner, which would be served in thirty minutes' time.

Mom and Mariah had decided that would be enough time for anyone not invited to the dinner to clear out, and for Mom to get a few last-minute pictures in place for the meal and following reception.

He ducked past the break in the corner of the tent, stepping out of the wedding tent and into the dinner tent. The staff had gathered there, and the head chef was leading a meeting about the food, the order of service, and the expectations for that afternoon.

Conrad felt very out of place, but he was used to such a thing. He stood quietly in the corner, no one looking his way at all, which was also about how things went.

Across from him, he could see several waitresses as he scanned, and then a face caught his attention in a way no other had.

He pulled in a breath as their eyes met, and he said right out loud, "You've got to be kidding me," when Ryanne Moon's eyes rounded as she recognized him.

Every eye in the tent turned toward him then, and the chef stopped talking. Conrad felt wind blowing through his soul, and he had to work extremely hard not to bark a question at Ryanne about what in the world she was doing here, dressed like that, when she should be in some slinky, sexy gown on his arm.

SNEAK PEEK! CHAPTER TWO - SAVING THE COWBOY BILLIONAIRE

Ryanne Moon's prayers had gone unanswered. In fact, the Lord had downright blown them up. He'd done the exact opposite of what she'd been asking him to do—keep her invisible that day. Keep Conrad's attention somewhere else.

He'd be sitting at the front of the tent, and she'd specifically requested the back section. She'd be wearing all black, and waiters and waitresses were invisible. No one truly looked at them. No one even cared they were there, unless their food didn't come out.

Why in the world was he standing in her staff meeting?

Not your staff, she had the wherewithal to think. She had a staff down the road, in a strip mall, in her clothing store. This was a job for a friend to whom she owed a favor. Wendell had called, and Ry hadn't been able to say no.

She didn't seem to have a problem telling Conrad Chappell no, though faced with him in that suit, with flowers pinned to the lapel, and every line hitting his muscular body in exactly the right way...and Ryanne wouldn't even be able to speak.

Chef Lucas Wendall pushed through the crowd to Conrad and said something Ryanne couldn't hear from clear across the tent. She couldn't see Conrad, as Wendell had plenty of bulk on his frame too.

He turned a few moments later and said, "Ryanne, I need you over here."

All the eyes shifted to her, and she prayed that the Lord would open up the Earth and swallow her whole with every step she took.

Just another prayer that went unanswered, as she arrived next to Wendell and in front of Conrad only a few seconds later.

"He needs to talk to you," Wendell said. "You know what you're doing, but I need you back in ten minutes."

"Yes, sir," she said, though Wendell was one of her oldest friends. Technically, he'd been Andrea's best friend growing up, but Ry had known him her whole life. After Andy's death, Ry and Wendell had found some comfort in each other, and if there was anyone Ry couldn't say no to when he was in a pinch, it was Wendell.

Conrad indicated the wide open tent to his left, and Ry followed him in that direction. Her heart lodged itself right up in her throat, and she wasn't sure how to speak and keep breathing at the same time.

Conrad led her through the maze of tables to the outer edge of the tent, as far from the staff meeting as he could get.

Cars and trucks had been parked along the lane in front of where the wedding events were taking place, as well as all the way down the dirt road that led toward a bend and back toward the main highway.

The Chappells had always known how to throw a good party.

"Remember when you guys hosted a New Year's Eve bash in the barn?" she asked, not sure why that particular memory had crept up on her. "It was our senior year."

"Yes," he said, his tone clipped and formal.

"I only came for a few minutes," she said. "I didn't stay until midnight or anything." She hadn't wanted to see Conrad kiss someone else, and he'd been there with his latest fling. She'd been the same age as them, and he'd found someone else by Valentine's Day.

No matter who he went out with, Ryanne hated that it wasn't her. She'd also learned that year that Conrad had wings, and she didn't think there was a woman alive who could clip them.

She wondered if that had changed in the years that had passed since then.

"It was a good party," he said. "Why'd you leave?"

She stared out at the blue sky, only a few wispy clouds floating through it. The air smelled half like the food she'd be serving soon and half like pure country. Sunshine, horses, and possibilities.

His sister-in-law should make a candle for that. *Pure country*.

Ryanne had done a little Internet digging of her own

since her date with Conrad last week. The Chappell brothers and Bluegrass Ranch did very well for themselves. This was the sixth brother to tie the knot, and one of his brothers had won the Sweetheart Classic twice in a row.

Olivia Hudson had won a major internship with a huge retailer that had taken her perfumery from a mom-and-pop operation she ran out of her garage to an international company that sold perfumes, colognes, and scented candles in all fifty states—and now thirteen countries.

Another brother had snagged himself an award-winning leatherworker for a wife, and Tamara Lennox was known all over the South for her fine craftsmanship.

They had the best wedding planner in the state now that Mariah had married Lawrence, and Lisa Harvey owned one of the most prestigious stud farms in the area.

It was Ginny Winters who really crowned the Chappell family. She was the sole heiress to Sweet Rose Whiskey, which had been in business for over a century, and who had more money than the Queen of England.

Conrad's parents were well-respected in the community, and his mother had been heading up charitable organizations for fifty years now.

Not only would Ryanne not fit in this prestigious family, she couldn't even imagine herself at family parties and get-togethers.

"Do you want me to be honest?" she asked. In her heart, she wanted him to say yes. She had things to say to him; things that wouldn't go away until she did.

"I would prefer that to a vague text about something coming up that you have to take care of," he said dryly. Maybe he was barely holding back his anger. She wasn't quite sure.

"Something *did* come up," she said. "Wendell needed servers for this wedding, and I've worked with him a lot."

"He was Andy's boyfriend," Conrad said.

"Yes."

"What about last Friday?"

Ryanne swallowed. "Last Friday was me freaking out," she said.

"About what?" Conrad tore his eyes from the horizon and looked at her. "I thought we had a great lunch on Wednesday. Well, at least after the part where I sort of yelled at you." He offered her a kind smile, and oh, she shouldn't have looked at him.

"We did," she said. "I...I'm so busy, Conrad. I just need to get Andy and Ryan off the ground. Then maybe we'd have a chance."

He studied her, and in high school, he'd simply accepted whatever she'd said to him. He could still hear her telling him on New Year's Eve that she needed to get home to help Tyler with his party. Conrad hadn't questioned why her older brother couldn't put on his own party without her help.

He was questioning her now, and he hadn't even said anything.

She looked away, sighing. If she stayed here much longer, she'd tell him too much, and then she'd regret everything about this day, not just that she wasn't wearing her designer gown and hanging on his arm.

"Why'd you leave the New Year's Eve party?" he asked. "Honestly."

"Honestly." She took a deep breath. "Because you were there with Annette Lansing, and I couldn't stand to see you kiss someone else when the clock struck midnight." She looked at him, everything laid out between them.

"Why'd you cancel on Friday?"

"Because," she said. "I knew if I started seeing you again, I'd fall in love with you, and you'd break my heart all over again." She whispered the last several words. Tears filled her eyes, but they weren't the happy kind people cried at weddings.

She brushed at her eyes quickly, because she didn't want to ruin her makeup. She had a job still to do today. "Please, Conrad. Just leave me alone, okay? I'm opening my store, and I'm finally feeling like a normal person after Andy died, and I need my heart."

A storm raged across Conrad's face. She hadn't known the man possessed such strong emotions; in high school, he had a devil-may-care attitude, and he'd been larger than life. She could still feel that energy pulsing off of him, and she knew she'd do dangerous things to be with him.

"What if I promised not to break your heart?" he asked, each word carefully measured out. He swallowed after the question, clearly having trouble keeping everything tightly controlled.

"How can you make such a promise?" She shook her

head, horrified when an errant tear splashed her cheek. She swiped at it and drew in a breath. "I have to get back to work. I'm sorry about Friday and today. I just need to focus, and Conrad, you've always been terrible for my focus."

"I'm not the same person I was in high school," he said.

"No," she said. "You're not. You're better."

He shook his head. "Not true. Please, don't say no all the way yet." He reached out and brushed her fingers with his. A whisper of a touch, the way she skimmed her hand across the tops of the blades of grass.

Instant heat filled her body, and Ryanne really wanted to say yes. "I can give you a halfway yes."

"I'll take it," he whispered, drawing her fully into his arms. He smelled like pine trees and leather, fresh air and a mountain fire. He'd always been the man of her dreams, and that hadn't changed about him. "I just want a chance."

He pulled away, his hands sliding down to her waist, where he held her as he looked at her. "Can you give me a chance to show you that I'm not the same? I'm not better, and I'm not worse. I'm just older. Different. I think we'd be really good together." Another swallow, and she liked that he was nervous. It made her feel more powerful than she otherwise would have.

She nodded, not sure what to say, and the next thing she knew, Conrad had placed one hand on the side of her face and lowered his mouth to touch hers.

She reacted like a dehydrated man who'd just found water, and she kissed him back with enthusiasm. She told herself that it was because she hadn't had a boyfriend in years. She hadn't kissed a man in so long.

Really, though, it was because he was Conrad Chappell, and she'd always failed at staying away from him.

* * *

I can't wait to see what will happen with Conrad and Ryanne in ***SAVING THE COWBOY BILLIONAIRE.***
You can read it right now in paperback.

BLUEGRASS RANCH ROMANCE

Book 1: Winning the Cowboy Billionaire: She'll do anything to secure the funding she needs to take her perfumery to the next level...even date the boy next door.

Book 2: Roping the Cowboy Billionaire: She'll do anything to show her ex she's not still hung up on him...even date her best friend.

Book 3: Training the Cowboy Billionaire: She'll do anything to save her ranch...even marry a cowboy just so they can enter a race together.

Book 4: Parading the Cowboy Billionaire: She'll do anything to spite her mother and find her own happiness...even keep her cowboy billionaire boyfriend a secret.

Book 5: Promoting the Cowboy Billionaire: She'll do anything to keep her job...even date a client to stay on her boss's good side.

Book 6: Acquiring the Cowboy Billionaire: She'll do anything to keep her father's stud farm in the family...even marry the maddening cowboy billionaire she's never gotten along with.

Book 7: Saving the Cowboy Billionaire: She'll do anything to prove to her friends that she's over her ex...even date the cowboy she once went with in high school.

Book 8: Convincing the Cowboy Billionaire: She'll do anything to keep her dignity...even convincing the saltiest cowboy billionaire at the ranch to be her boyfriend.

CHESTNUT RANCH ROMANCE

Book 1: A Cowboy and his Neighbor: Best friends and neighbors shouldn't share a kiss...

Book 2: A Cowboy and his Mistletoe Kiss: He wasn't supposed to kiss her. Can Travis and Millie find a way to turn their mistletoe kiss into true love?

Book 3: A Cowboy and his Christmas Crush: Can a Christmas crush and their mutual love of rescuing dogs bring them back together?

Book 4: A Cowboy and his Daughter: They were married for a few months. She lost their baby...or so he thought.

Book 5: A Cowboy and his Boss: She's his boss. He's had a crush on her for a couple of summers now. Can Toni and Griffin mix business and pleasure while making sure the teens they're in charge of stay in line?

Book 6: A Cowboy and his Fake Marriage: She needs a husband to keep her ranch...can she convince the cowboy next-door to marry her?

Book 7: A Cowboy and his Secret Kiss: He likes the pretty adventure guide next door, but she wants to keep their relationship off the grid. Can he kiss her in secret and keep his heart intact?

Book 8: A Cowboy and his Skipped Christmas: He's been in love with her forever. She's told him no more times than either of them can count. Can Theo and Sorrell find their way through past pain to a happy future together?

Texas Longhorn Ranch Romance

Book 1: Loving Her Cowboy Best Friend: She's a city girl returning to her hometown. He's a country boy through and through. When these two former best friends (and ex-lovers) start working together, romantic sparks fly that could ignite a wildfire... Will Regina and Blake get burned or can they tame the flames into true love?

Book 2: Kissing Her Cowboy Boss: She's a veterinarian with a secret past. He's her new boss. When Todd hires Laura, it's because she's willing to live on-site and work full-time for the ranch. But when their feelings turn personal, will Laura put up walls between them to keep them apart?

Book 3: Claiming Her Cowboy Kiss: He's tried and failed in country music - and women - before. She wasn't supposed to be at the ranch that summer. When Maddy shows up unexpectedly, will she and Kyle have their second chance romance? Or will the call of the stage lure him away?

Book 4: Dreaming of Her Cowboy Prince: She works constantly, never really leaving the family ranch where she's the evening manager. He's not who he says he is... Can Holly and Silas find their way through their troubles at the Texas Longhorn Ranch to a happily-ever-after?

About Emmy

Emmy is a Midwest mom who loves dogs, cowboys, and Texas. She's been writing for years and loves weaving stories of love, hope, and second chances. Learn more about her and her books at www.feelgoodfictionbooks.com.

CPSIA information can be obtained
at www.ICGtesting.com
Printed in the USA
BVHW041427140623
665887BV00008B/873